"Nick, don't

"Don't what? Don't remember the past? Don't admire the gorgeous woman you've become?"

The heat in his eyes scorched her, captivated her, held her spellbound.

"Or don't do something as crazy as this?"

Before she could blink, he hauled her into his arms and kissed her.

The kisses they'd shared as teenagers had been exploratory, tender and achingly poignant. Yet there was nothing remotely sweet or gentle about his mouth crushing hers now.

Their lips clashed in a frantic, hungry union, a fusion of tongues, a meshing of desire that left her reeling.

She should have been immune to him by now. She should have pushed him away and laughed it off as a quick reacquainting peck between friends for old times' sake.

Should have, should have, should have… As she stood on tiptoes, leaned into him and wrapped her arms around his neck, her resolve to push him away melted—just as it had ten years earlier when she'd acted on all the bottled-up feelings she'd harbored for him for years.

Dear Presents Reader,

Happy Valentine's Day—and if you're in the mood for hot steamy romance, look no further than these exciting new stories from the Harlequin Presents® line! Two books a month that offer you all that you expect from Presents—but with a sassy, sexy, flirty attitude!

All year you'll find these exciting new books from an array of vibrant, sparkling authors such as Kate Hardy, Heidi Rice, Kimberly Lang, Natalie Anderson and Robyn Grady. This month there's sizzle and sass from talented new Atlanta author Kimberly Lang with *Magnate's Mistress...Accidentally Pregnant!* And for sun, sea and sex, don't miss *Marriage: For Business or Pleasure?* by Australian author Nicola Marsh.

Next month, there's the first in Kelly Hunter's saucy new duet, HOT BED OF SCANDAL, set on a French vineyard and entitled *Exposed: Misbehaving with the Magnate.* And there's an exciting and dramatic pregnancy story from hot British talent Heidi Rice in *Public Affair, Secretly Expecting.*

We'd love to hear what you think of these novels—why not drop us a line at Presents@hmb.co.uk.

With best wishes,

The Editors

Nicola Marsh

MARRIAGE: FOR BUSINESS OR PLEASURE?

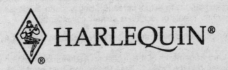

HARLEQUIN®

TORONTO • NEW YORK • LONDON
AMSTERDAM • PARIS • SYDNEY • HAMBURG
STOCKHOLM • ATHENS • TOKYO • MILAN • MADRID
PRAGUE • WARSAW • BUDAPEST • AUCKLAND

ISBN-13: 978-0-373-12898-3

MARRIAGE: FOR BUSINESS OR PLEASURE?

First North American Publication 2010.

www.eHarlequin.com

Printed in U.S.A.

All about the author...
Nicola Marsh

NICOLA MARSH has always had a passion for writing and reading. As a youngster, she devoured books when she should have been sleeping, and she later kept a diary that could be an epic in itself! These days, when she's not enjoying life with her husband and son in her home city of Melbourne, she's at her computer doing her dream job—creating the romances she loves. Visit Nicola's Web site at www.nicolamarsh.com for the latest news of her books.

Nicola also writes for Harlequin® Romance.

With thanks to Laurie Schnebly, for being a great teacher and for getting me to ask my characters *why?*

CHAPTER ONE

THE rented SUV swerved on the dusty, potholed driveway of the Mancini place and Brittany Lloyd bit back a curse.

Her average driving skills had little to do with the state of the road or the unwelcome memories assailing her and everything to do with the naked man bent over a thresher.

Semi-naked, technically, as her gaze riveted to the tantalising expanse of bronze, broad back glistening in the scorching Queensland sun.

The muscles shifted, bunched, slid, as he straightened and thrust hands into back pockets of ripped, faded denim, and as her greedy gaze strayed to his butt she suddenly wished she hadn't stayed away so long.

Ten years in London had been a sane choice, a safe choice considering what she'd been running from, but seeing this hot guy on her first morning home reinforced no place on earth bred guys like Jacaranda.

She should know.

She'd fallen in love with one, had given him her heart, her virginity and her loyalty.

More fool her.

As she righted the car and approached, the guy half turned and this time the SUV sheered straight off the driveway and almost straight into a ditch.

The engine stalled, spluttered, died, as her white-knuckled hands gripped the steering wheel, shock and joy and mind-numbing lust slamming into her, leaving her powerless to do anything but watch *him* approach.

Not a flicker of emotion crossed Nick Mancini's face as he reached the car, leaned tanned, toned forearms on the open window and gave her a casual nod.

'Hey, Britt. Long time no see.'

A casual greeting, without rancour or bitterness; then again, she'd been the one left to pick up the pieces when he'd ended it.

The greeting and his lack of emotion didn't do justice to what they'd shared, what they'd given up and she'd be damned if she showed him anything other than the same lackadaisi-cal nonchalance despite her jack-hammering heart and clammy hands.

'Ten years, give or take.'

She wanted him to acknowledge the time they'd spent apart, wanted him to ask how she'd been, wanted him to finally explain why he'd opted out.

Instead, he shrugged, her gaze drifting to those bunching muscles of their own volition, all too aware of how he'd filled out in the last ten years.

He'd been lean rather than muscular back then and now... She wrenched her gaze away from his impressive pecs and focused on his face.

Nick the teenager had been good-looking, cocky and a rebel.

Nick the man was drop-dead gorgeous in a rough-around-the-edges way, still cocky and, if she read him right, still out to prove to the world he didn't give a damn.

By the smug grin lifting the corners of an all too kissable mouth, she'd read him just right.

'What brings you by?'

'Business.'

Something solid, tangible and guaranteed to keep errant

emotions at bay no matter how much she wanted to ask him 'what the hell happened to us?'

She'd hoped to avoid him, had hoped to do business with his father but she'd been a fool. This place was in Nick's veins, of course he'd be here doing a hard day's work, working longer and tougher and harder than all his employees.

'Business, huh?'

His caramelised-toffee eyes narrowed and she wished he'd stop staring at her as if she had a dirt smudge on her nose. He'd always had the ability to see into her soul and right now that was the last thing she needed.

She needed to stay focused. Her promotion depended on it.

'I've got a proposition for you.'

He straightened, all six feet two of lean, hard muscle, and smiled that bad-boy smile she remembered so well, the smile that had haunted her for months when she'd first arrived in London, pining away for her first love—the same love who had turned down her offer to come with her, to build a life together.

'I just bet you have, Red.'

He opened the car door and she stepped out, wishing she could hide her blush, knowing it would do nothing for her freckles and hating herself for caring so damn much.

'No one's called me that in years,' she muttered, thankful her hair bore more coppery-blonde streaks these days than the fire-engine red she'd grown up with.

'That's a shame.'

He reached out, twisted a stray strand around his finger.

'They obviously don't know you as well as I do.'

She pulled away quickly before she did something stupid, such as stand there and let him twist her around his finger and not just by the hair. 'You don't know me at all.'

Ignoring the glint in his eyes, which seemed a richer, deeper toffee than she remembered, she glanced at her watch, hoping he'd get the hint.

'Is your father here? I need to discuss this with him.'

His eyes clouded, darkened, as pain twisted his mouth. 'Papa died. Guess the news didn't make it all the way to London.'

'I'm sorry,' she said, suddenly ashamed she hadn't kept in touch with news from home.

Not that the thought hadn't crossed her mind on occasion but then, he hadn't been the reason she'd fled Jacaranda.

'Are you really?'

She noticed the angry lines fanning from the corner of his mouth, the indentation between his brows, aging him beyond his twenty-eight years.

He'd never looked at her like this back then. Uh-uh. He might have been a rebel but he'd never been brooding or angry, far from it.

A decade earlier he'd only ever looked at her with adoration and desire, and for a brief moment she wished she could turn back time.

'Of course I'm sorry. Everyone around here loved Papa.'

'You're right.'

Swiping a hand across his face, he erased the tenseness. 'Though I'm surprised your old man didn't say something. You can't ride a Harley in this town without people lining the roads for a parade.'

His gaze flicked over her and she clenched her hands to stop from smoothing her Dolce and Gabbana suit. His eyes glowed with appreciation but she didn't miss the slight compression of his lips, as if her favourite designer suit didn't impress him one bit.

'Despite your fancy new clothes, surely you remember how it is around here?'

He was trying to bait her, just as he always did and, damn him, she wouldn't give him the satisfaction of knowing exactly how much she remembered, most of her memories centred on him.

'I've been busy the last ten years so forgive me if taking a stroll down memory lane hasn't been high on my list of priorities.'

'Busy, huh?'

She expected him to ask about her career, wanted to show him how far she'd come, how far they could've made it as a couple if he'd accompanied her.

Instead, he stood there, a semi-naked god totally at ease with his surroundings, the sheen of sweat and dust adding to his rugged appeal rather than diminishing it.

Clamping down on the mental image to run her hands over that glorious bare chest, she cleared her throat.

'I work twenty-four-seven. Being a senior exec at London's top advertising company takes up most of my time.'

'What, no time for play?'

His teasing smile slammed into her, the familiarity of it making her gasp.

She didn't play, not any more. Her play days had stopped when she'd hightailed it out of this town and never looked back.

Work helped her forget…everything.

Work proved how far she'd come.

Work gave her the hard-fought independence she'd clawed her way to the top for, an independence that guaranteed she'd never have to look back.

Biting back a pithy retort, she ducked into the car and grabbed the Manila folder from the passenger seat.

'What I do in my spare time isn't your concern. I'm here on business.'

'Whatever this business proposition of yours is about, you'll be dealing with me.'

He fixed her with a probing stare, a potent stare that sent a ripple of unease through her.

'And just so you know, I'm nothing like my father. I drive a hard bargain.'

She almost banged her head on the door jamb as his silky

voice slid over her. So much for a quick, clean presentation to Papa Mancini. The thought of doing business with Nick, let alone considering whatever bargain he might demand, had her flustered.

And she never got flustered, not any more. Some of the gang at work called her the Ice Princess behind her back and she liked it. Emotions got her nowhere and she'd learned to control her fiery temper along with the rest of her wayward emotions during the long, hard graft in the big city.

As she handed him the folder their fingertips touched and despite the length of time they'd been apart, her heart jack-knifed. Wretched organ. She shouldn't feel anything where Nick was concerned, especially not this strange déjà vu that had her dreaming of stepping closer and running a palm down his bare chest to see if it felt half as good as she remembered.

She took a steadying breath, ignoring the host of unwelcome feelings this man resurrected.

'There's a lot we need to discuss. Why don't we head inside so you can put on some clothes and we can do business?'

She'd made a fatal error in judgement, knew it the second his lips kicked up into a sexy, familiar grin that never failed to take her breath away.

She shouldn't have mentioned his state of undress, shouldn't have drawn attention to it, and as if of their own volition her eyes drifted south, riveted to that muscular expanse of temptation less than two feet away.

He was so bronze, so broad, so breathtaking and when she finally dragged her gaze away her knees shook.

'You sure you want me to get dressed?'

Damn him, he'd called her on her faux pas. A gentleman would've ignored her slip-up. Then again, since when had Nick been a gentleman?

Jacaranda's answer to James Dean had had girls swooning and fathers reaching for shotguns since he'd hit puberty and she was a fool for expecting anything other than bluntness from the guy who'd once rocked her world.

'Nick, don't.'

She held up a hand, about as effective as a cockatoo trying to ward off a charging emu.

'Don't what?'

He stared at her hand as if he wanted to grab it and she quickly let it drop.

'Don't remember the past? Don't admire the gorgeous woman you've become?'

The heat in his eyes scorched her, captivated her, held her spellbound.

'Or don't do something as crazy as this?'

Before she could blink, he hauled her into his arms and kissed her.

The kisses they'd shared as teenagers had been exploratory, tender and achingly poignant. Yet there was nothing remotely sweet or gentle about his mouth crushing hers now.

Their lips clashed in a frantic, hungry union, a fusion of tongues, a meshing of desire that left her reeling.

She should've been immune to him by now. She should've pushed him away and laughed it off as a quick reacquainting peck between friends for old times' sake.

Should've, should've, should've, as she stood on tiptoes, leaned into him and wrapped her arms around his neck, hanging on as if her life depended on it.

As he softened the kiss, plying her with a skilled precision he'd never had as a young man, her resolve to push him away melted, just as it had ten years earlier when she'd acted on all the bottled-up feelings she'd harboured for him for years.

She'd idolised him all through the endless teenage years and he hadn't glanced in her direction until she'd turned eighteen, thrown herself at him and been wonderfully surprised when the bad boy of Jacaranda had returned her interest.

They'd gone steady for exactly six months before things had come to a head at home and she'd been forced to flee.

She hadn't told Nick about her humiliation, wanting him to need her for who she was, not following her out of some warped sense of pity. So she'd tried to convince him to run away with her. And she'd failed. Not just failed, he'd pushed her away with a callousness that had shattered her heart.

So what the heck was she doing, kissing him like this?

As her common sense belatedly kicked in Nick broke the kiss, untangling her hands from behind his neck and setting them firmly at her side before glaring at her, as if she'd been the one to instigate their clinch in the first place.

'Don't expect me to be sorry for that,' he said, running a hand through his dark wavy hair, sending it in all directions.

'I gave up expecting anything from you a long time ago.'

She shrugged, aiming for nonchalant while her insides churned, and ran a finger along her bottom lip, wondering if it looked as bruised as it felt.

He'd kissed her…and she'd liked it!

So much for the Ice Princess. Looked as if her hard-fought emotion-free veneer had melted the minute he'd lip-locked her.

Nick muttered a curse and turned away from Brittany before he made another blunder and hauled her right back into his arms.

She felt good, better than he remembered and he had a damn good memory when it came to this woman.

She'd been the one for him.

And he'd sent her away.

He'd had no choice, but a day hadn't gone by when he hadn't replayed memories of the red-haired hellion who'd captured his heart without trying.

Here she was, just as incredible as he remembered.

And he was drawn to her as uncontrollably as ever. For the

spell she'd cast over him had never been simply caused by her blue eyes, porcelain skin and waist-length auburn hair that begged a guy to run his fingers through it. Nor did it have anything to do with her lithe body, with enough curves to turn a guy's head.

No, Brittany Lloyd possessed a more elusive charm, something that drew him surer than spicy tomato meatballs.

Class.

Something he'd craved his entire life, something he'd set about gaining the last few years but she'd been born with, and no amount of mixing in the right circles or business success could buy what she had, in spades.

'About this business proposition?' He turned back to face her, surprised by the vulnerability he glimpsed in her eyes. Hell, it was just a damn kiss, no big deal.

'All in there.'

She pointed at the Manila folder in his hands, stared at it as if it were a ticking bomb ready to detonate.

He weighed it in one hand, tapped it against his palm, gauging her reaction.

'Jeez, why don't you just open it?' She exploded, just as she used to in the good old days and he grinned.

'Good to see you've still got that fiery temper beneath all that polish.'

He looked her up and down, admiring the subtle changes to her appearance: the gold streaks in her now shoulder-length hair, the svelte body packed with more curves than a racetrack, the elegant wardrobe. As a teenager she'd been pretty. As a woman, she was stunning.

With a confident toss of that luscious hair, she fixed him with a newly acquired haughty grin.

'Actually, you're the only one who seems to bring it out in me. Now, back to business?'

Curiosity ate at him. To bring her back here, this precious

business deal of hers had to be important. In that case, he wanted to be one hundred per cent appraised of the situation before he started discussing anything with her.

He raised an eyebrow, rattled the folder and gestured at his bare torso. 'I don't do business like this. Where are you staying?'

To his delight, she blushed, her gaze lingering on his chest a few seconds too long. 'The Phant-A-Sea in Noosa.'

Oh, this just got better and better.

'But I don't expect you to drive all that way just to meet me. We can do this here—'

'I was heading into town after I'd finished up here anyway. Why don't I meet you there around five? We can discuss this over drinks.'

'That won't be necessary—'

'But it will.'

He leaned closer, her awareness of him evident in the widening of her pupils, the tip of her tongue darting out to moisten her bottom lip, and his gut clenched with how badly he still wanted her.

Maybe he should tell her the truth now and be done with it.

But then, where was the fun in that?

'Give me some time to clean up, take a look at your proposal and we can discuss it over a Shirley Temple.'

He scored another direct hit with reference to her favourite drink back then, her lips compressing into an unimpressed line.

'This isn't some trip down memory lane. This is business.'

His glance strayed to her lips, lush and pouting, before sweeping back to her eyes, registering the shock of arousal that made a mockery of their *business*.

'So you keep saying. Business. Ri-i-ight.'

To his surprise, she laughed. 'You haven't changed a bit. Still the charmer.'

She was wrong, dead wrong.

He'd changed and, come five o'clock, she'd discover exactly how much.

Propping on the bonnet, he crossed his ankles. 'Is it working?'

'Nope, I'm immune to rebel charmers these days.'

'Pity.'

His glance slid over her, taking in every delicious curve, earning another blush.

'How long are you in town for?'

'For as long as it takes.'

She'd gone cold again. Retreating back into the business at hand...

His glance swept the distant cane fields he loved so much, encompassing the sugar cane that was as much a part of him as his Italian heritage, wondering what she'd make of him once she discovered *his* real business these days.

Would she be impressed? Probably, though in all fairness what he did or where he came from had never been an issue with her.

They'd been friends before lovers in the old days, travelling on the same bus to school every day even though she'd attended the private grammar school and he'd gone to the local high school.

She'd pretended to ignore him at first so he'd done his best to rile her with constant taunts about everything from her shiny shoes to her long red pigtails. And when her fiery temper had sparked her into retaliating by ramming his bike with hers, their friendship had been cemented.

She'd never given a damn about the gaping hole in their social circles: the richest girl in the district hooking up with the Italian working-class farm boy.

But other people had. He'd heard the whispers, the innuendos, about her slumming it with him before she got married to a suitable man.

He'd let it taint what they had, had ended it for good

before things got out of control. But he'd never forgotten how dating her had made him feel. Simply, he'd wanted to be a better man for her.

All ancient history, and as he refocused he knew that impulsive kiss was a stupid move.

He didn't do impulsive any more. Every decision he made was carefully weighed, evaluated and executed with the utmost precision. He wasn't at the top of his game these days for nothing.

Pushing off the car, he tapped the bonnet.

'You better get going. Give me a chance to finish up here and meet you later.'

'Fine.'

He opened the car door for her and watched as she buckled up. Déjà vu hit and an irresistible impulse came over him in spite of all the resolutions he'd just made. He leaned in quickly through the open window.

'Hey, Red?'

'Yeah?'

He grinned and tweaked her nose just as he used to. 'You kiss even better than I remember.'

Before she could respond, he straightened, chuckling at the instant indignation sparking her beautiful eyes as he strode towards the farmhouse.

CHAPTER TWO

BRITTANY pressed her hands to her flushed cheeks as Nick strode away.

The man was a menace.

In less than ten minutes he'd managed to unbalance her, unhinge her and undermine her.

As for that kiss…she thunked her head on the steering wheel, twice, for good measure.

Not only had she stood there and let him do it, she'd responded! Like a woman who hadn't been kissed in a very long time.

Which in all honesty was probably true considering she'd been so focused on the managing director position coming up for grabs she hadn't dated in yonks.

But that didn't excuse her eager response, nor did the total and utter meltdown she'd experienced the second his lips had touched hers.

'Ice Princess my butt,' she muttered, releasing the brake and sending gravel flying before heading back down the drive.

Sneaking a peek in the rear-vision mirror, she wasn't surprised to see Nick staring over his shoulder with a grin as wide as the Sydney Harbour Bridge plastered across his smug face.

She clamped her lips shut on a host of expletives and headed for the main highway.

In a way, she was glad he'd suggested they meet at her hotel to discuss her proposal. She'd be much better prepared to face him again in the cool elegance of the Phant-A-Sea's front bar than inside the cosy farmhouse that held a host of memories.

Wonderful, heartfelt memories of sitting across from him at the handmade wooden dining table, tearing into steaming *ciabatta* hot from the oven, dipping it into olive oil and balsamic vinegar, licking the drips off each other's fingers...

Cuddling up on the worn chintz sofa, watching old black and white Laurel and Hardy movies and laughing themselves silly.

Clearing the family room of its mismatched lounge chairs and scarred coffee table stacked with newspapers and magazines so they could dance body to body to their favourite crooning country singer.

The memories were so real, so poignant that her eyes misted over and she blinked, caught up in the magic of the past when she should be focused on the future.

Her future as Managing Director of Sell depended on it.

Come five o'clock, she'd make sure Nick Mancini with his sexy smile and flashing dimples and hot body knew exactly the type of businesswoman he was dealing with.

Brittany sipped at her sugar-cane juice as she glanced around the Phant-A-Sea's bar.

She'd stayed in some gorgeous hotels around the world but this one was something else. From its sandstone-tiled entrance to its pristine whitewashed exterior, from its cascading waterfalls to the stunning umbrella-shaped poincianas lush with flamboyant crimson flowers, it beckoned a weary traveller to come in and stay awhile.

As for her beautiful room with its king-size bed and six-hundred-thread-count sheets, double shower, Jacuzzi and locally made lavender toiletries, she could happily stay there for ever.

But this wasn't a pleasure trip, far from it.

She needed to seal this deal with Nick. It would give her confidence an added boost to face the other nemesis this journey: her father.

They hadn't spoken in ten years.

But she was here, he now lived in an exclusive special accommodation for the elderly and, as she wouldn't be back, she needed to put the past to rest, say a proper good-bye this time.

She'd taken up yoga in London, was a convert to karma, and wanted to ensure hers was good rather than being dogged the rest of her life for not doing the right thing when she had the opportunity.

Swirling the lime wedge in her juice around and around, she mulled over her dad's anger, his need to control, his escalating abuse before she'd left.

He'd always been domineering but when she'd turned eighteen he'd gone into overdrive. She'd escaped, hadn't looked back, but there wasn't a day went by when she hadn't wondered how different her life would've been if she'd stuck around.

Would she and Nick have married? Would they have a brood of gorgeous, curly dark-haired, dimpled kids?

Swallowing the lump of regret clogging her throat, she glanced up, and the lump expanded to Ayers Rock proportions.

Farm-boy Nick in faded, torn denim and sweat-glistening chest was hot.

Executive Nick in an ebony pinstriped designer suit, crisp white shirt accentuating his tan and a silk amethyst tie was something else entirely.

She froze as he strode towards her, all long legs and designer outfit and dimpled smile.

'Hope you haven't been waiting long.'

He ducked his head to plant a quick kiss on her cheek and

her senses reeled as she caught the faintest whiff of his familiar woody deodorant mingled with the sweetness of harvested cane.

Memories slammed into her: snuggling in the crook of his arm under *their* jacaranda tree, lying on top of him along the river bank, nuzzling his neck as they made love… She gulped a lungful of air, several, to ease her breathlessness.

His scent was so evocative, so rich in memories she struggled to remember what he'd just asked her.

Casting a curious glance her way, he sat opposite, his knees in close proximity to hers, and she surreptitiously sidled back to avoid accidental contact.

That was all she needed. As if she hadn't made enough of a fool of herself already.

'What do you think of the hotel?'

She managed to unglue her tongue from the roof of her mouth, take a quick sip of her juice before answering. 'It's gorgeous. There was nothing like it ten years ago.'

His proud grin baffled her as much as seeing him in a suit. 'Phant-A-Sea was built five years ago. Business is booming.'

Taking in the subtle lighting, the understated elegance, she nodded.

'I'm not surprised. I've travelled extensively for business the last six years or so, but haven't stayed in anything quite like this before.'

The mention of business cleared the sensual fog that had enveloped her the moment he'd strutted into the bar, and she glanced at his empty hands.

'Where's my proposal? Did you take a look at it?'

He shook his head, gestured to a waiter who scurried over as if the prime minister had beckoned.

'I prefer to hear this pitch from you first, then go over the details later.'

'Is that why you're in a suit?' she blurted, wishing she

adn't asked when his gaze raked over her own change of
lothes. The dove-grey skirt suit was another favourite, never
iiled to give her a confidence boost and with Nick's steamy
:are sliding over her she needed every ounce of confidence
ie could get.

Before he could respond, the waiter said, 'The usual, Mr
Mancini?'

'Yes, thanks, Kyoshi.'

Confused, she flicked her gaze between the two. Nick
adn't as much as glanced at the waiter's name tag, and along
vith 'the usual' it was obvious he frequented this place.

Strange, considering thriving, cosmopolitan Noosa was a
ood ninety-minute drive from the plantation and she hadn't
egged Nick for the bar-hopping type.

Then again, she'd been away a decade, people changed, so
vhat did she know?

'You like?'

He glanced down at his suit, leaving her no option but to
o the same, and she gulped at the way his chest filled out
ie shirt, how the fine material of the suit jacket hugged his
houlders.

'I've never seen you in one.'

His eyes glittered with a satisfaction she didn't understand
s he pinned her with a stare that had her squirming.

'Times change.'

She gripped her glass so tight she wouldn't have been at
ll surprised if it cracked and she forced her hand to relax and
lace it on the table by her elbow.

'They do. So let's get down to business.'

Leaning back, he placed an outstretched arm on the back
f his chair, the simple action pulling his shirt taut across the
uuscular chest she'd seen in all its glory earlier that day and
he instantly wished for a drink refill to cool her down.

'I have to say I'm intrigued. This business must be pretty

damn special to drag you back here from the bright lights
of London.'

Special? How could she begin to explain to him what this
promotion meant? The long hours she'd put in over the years?
The overnight jaunts to godforsaken places, going the extra
yards to secure information, ensuring her pitches were bigger
and better than everyone else's? The endless drive to prove
her independence in every way that counted?

Nick wouldn't get it.

Papa Mancini had doted on him, not having a mum had
bonded them like nothing else. Wish she could've said the
same for her 'family'.

'I'll give you the short version.'

She leaned forward, clasped her hands in her lap and
prepared to give the pitch of her life.

Securing the use of the Mancini plantation was paramount
to her plans and would assure her that promotion. The current
MD had virtually said so. Then why the nagging doubt convincing Nick wouldn't be as easy as she'd hoped?

'I work for Sell, London's biggest advertising company.
We're doing a worldwide campaign for the sugar industry
driven by the mega-wealthy plantation owners in the States.'

A flicker of interest lit his eyes and she continued. 'I'll be
honest with you, Nick. There's a big promotion in this for me,
a huge one. If I nail this, I'm the new managing director.'

His eyebrows shot up. 'That's some title.'

Picking up the boutique beer the waiter had discreetly
placed on the table in front of him, he took a healthy slug.

'So where do I fit into all this?'

She'd got this far. Taking a deep breath, she went for broke.

'Your place is the oldest sugar-cane plantation in Australia.
If I could have exclusive access to it, shoot footage, use some
of the history, I'm pretty sure the promotion is mine. That's
it in a nutshell.'

She didn't like his silence, his controlled posture. She'd expected some kind of reaction, not this tense quiet that left her on edge and wondering what was going on behind those deep dark eyes.

'I've set out facts and figures in the written proposal. How much the company's willing to pay to use the farm, how many hours it will involve, that kind of thing.'

Her voice had taken on a fake, bubbly edge, as if she was trying too hard, and she eventually fell silent, waiting for him to say something.

When he didn't, she blurted, 'Well, what do you think?'

Something shifted in his eyes, a shrewdness she'd never seen before.

'All sounds very feasible.'

Elation swept through her, quickly tempered when he leaned forward and shook his head.

'There's just one problem. I'm about to sell the farm.'

'Sell it? But where will you live? Where will you work?'

His condescending grin sent a chill of foreboding through her.

'You still see me as some hick bumpkin farm boy, don't you?'

She fought a rising blush and lost. 'Of course not. I just meant that place has been in your family for generations. I don't get why you'd sell now.'

He gestured all around him. 'Because my place is here now.'

Confusion creased her brow as she followed his hand. His designer suit, his patronising smile, his cryptic comments, made her feel as if she was left out of some in-joke and the punchline was on her.

'You belong here?'

She shook her head, knowing if there was one place a guy like Nick belonged, it wasn't in this ultra-elegant hotel.

He'd always loved the farm, had been proud of his family's heritage, so what had changed? The Nick she'd known and loved thrived under the harsh Queensland sun, harvesting billets of sugar cane, getting his hands dirty with the machinery he'd loved tinkering with, riding down the highway on his beat-up Harley with the wind in his hair and the devil at his back.

He frowned, his shoulders rigid as he sat back. 'You find that so hard to believe?'

'It's just not you.'

'It is now,' he snapped, his control slipping as anger flashed like fire from those dark eyes she'd lost herself in too many times to count.

'Just because we had a teenage fling, don't presume you know me.'

That hurt, more than she could've thought possible after all this time

'It was more than that and you know it.'

Understanding warred with passion before he blinked, obliterating the slightest sign he acknowledged what she'd said as true.

'Irrelevant to our business now.'

He glanced at his watch and stood up. 'Sorry, I have to cut this meeting short. I've got an interview scheduled.'

'You want to work here?'

He shrugged, the corners of his mouth twitching.

'I already do.'

'What?'

Thankfully, some of her old Ice Princess skills kicked in and prevented her jaw from hitting the floor.

'Though technically, that's not entirely right.'

Scanning his face, looking for a clue to what this was all about, she came up lacking.

'I don't understand.'

As he nodded to someone over her shoulder and held up a finger to indicate a minute he leaned down, his breath fanning her ear and sending ripples of heat through her. 'I don't just work here, I own the place.'

This time, as he strode away, she was sure her jaw did hit the floor.

Nick stared out of his office window on the fifth floor of the Phant-A-Sea, blind to the exquisite view of Noosa beach stretching into national park to the far right.

He'd loved this view when he'd first built the hotel, experienced a sense of immense satisfaction every time he'd sat behind this desk and stared out of the window.

Not today.

Today, whether his eyes were open or shut, all he could see was Britt's brilliant blue eyes wide with shock as he dropped his bombshell.

He'd expected to feel powerful, proud, even smug, when he told her the truth. So why the let-down, as if he should've come clean from the start?

What kind of game was he playing anyway? He didn't have time for them, not these days. On the verge of opening the fifth Phant-A-Sea hotel on Pink Sand Beach in the Bahamas and trying to build clientele here, he didn't have enough hours in the day.

That was why he was selling the farm. At least, that was his excuse and he was sticking to it.

He loved that place, had loved it from the first time Papa handed him a piece of sugar cane to gnaw on as a toddler, and it was as much a part of him as his love of the sea.

But that was part of the problem.

No one around these parts took him seriously as long as he was still connected to it, as long as every time they saw him they saw the rebel farm boy he used to be.

While the Phant-A-Sea was doing big business, he wanted

to expand, diversify, take his business to the next level and to
do so he needed investors.

If he didn't have the respect and backing of local investors
because of his heritage, what hope did he have with the
overseas moneymen?

Throw in the constant rumours about his reputation, label-
ling him as some Casanova playboy who couldn't possibly be
serious about business while playing the field, and he was
facing an uphill battle.

Not that it daunted him. He'd fought his way to where he
was today, had earned an MBA at night while slogging on the
farm trying to make a go of it during the days, had worked
damn hard to ensure a thriving cane plantation and the biggest,
brightest hotel Noosa had seen in years.

He'd fight now too, would show the investors he wasn't
some cocky upstart who'd lucked into the hotel business.

Yet the fact he had to part with a piece of his history, a piece
of his soul, to prove himself cut deep.

There had to be something else he could do…

Suddenly, he sat bolt upright, a ludicrous, crazy, just plain
loco idea shimmering at the edge of his consciousness.

He shoved it away, ignored it.

It didn't bear thinking about, wasn't worth entertaining for
one second.

Yet the more he tried to condemn the idea, the harder it
came, gnawing at him, demanding to be recognised as a valid
solution to his problem.

Slamming his silver ballpoint onto the desk, he pushed away
and strode to the window, planting his palms on the sill and
dropping his head forward until it hit the glass with a dull thud.

Questo è pazzia.

Papa had used the phrase often and it now echoed in his
head, 'this is crazy, this is crazy', making him feel the same
way when he'd been caught sneaking a smoke at ten, stealing

a kiss from a worker's wife at twelve and losing his virginity to a farmhand's sister at fourteen.

Hell, there'd be no way he'd be contemplating something as crazy as this if Papa were alive. The old man had been his conscience in more ways than one.

But Papa wasn't around any more and he owed it to him, to himself, to make the Mancini name one to be reckoned with, to bring recognition for a lifetime's hard work.

Contraccambio. Quid pro quo.

Britt wanted something from him, he wanted something in return.

But would she go for his proposal?

A simple business proposition, something she understood only too well if she'd travelled all this way for the sake of a promotion.

Yet what he had in mind was so...so...

Brilliant.

The businessman in him couldn't fault his proposition, whereas the carefree guy who'd fallen for a red-headed vixen the second he'd first laid eyes on her all those years ago knew that executing his plan wouldn't be simple at all.

CHAPTER THREE

BRITTANY gritted her teeth and rapped at Nick's door.

She'd been summoned.

Of all the nerve…if her promotion weren't so important she would've told him exactly where he could shove his summons.

But the promotion was all that mattered, why she was here, determined to keep a smile on her face and a lid on her curiosity no matter how much she wanted to know how Nick the bad boy had become Nick the billionaire.

The way he'd toyed with her, had dropped the information he was now a hotelier, rankled too, as if it had been one big game to him.

Well, screw him. And his four world-class hotels.

At least she'd come to this meeting prepared. After he'd dropped his little bombshell in the hotel bar she'd hightailed it back to her room and done a quick Internet search on the Phant-A-Sea chain.

What she'd discovered had blown her away.

Nick's hotels were luxury all the way, five-star elegance and beyond. Their breathtaking bedrooms were a signature feature, but all the reviews out there agreed that these classy hotels delivered on their promise—they were a fantasy experience all the way.

She'd been intrigued by the mention of a Caesar room, a

Casino Royale room and a Cinderella room, wishing there were pictures to go with the tempting descriptions.

Then again, if she played her cards right, maybe she'd get a first hand look at some of the rooms?

The thought of stepping inside the Jungle Safari room with Nick acting as tour guide brought a scorching blush to her cheeks and she pressed her hands against them, desperately trying to cool them before he opened the door and caught her on the back foot again.

The door swung open and she immediately squared her shoulders, ready for battle.

She'd left home at eighteen, travelled to the other side of the world, lived in a strange city and made a success of her life without using a penny of her father's money.

Making this deal happen with Nick should be a walk in Hyde Park, regardless of the games he seemed determined to play.

'Right on time.'

He stepped aside and gestured her into the room, a huge suite converted into an office, complete with monstrous mahogany desk, leather director's chair and a matching black leather lounge suite designed to make whoever set foot in the giant room at home.

She ignored the comfy-looking sofa and settled for the solitary chair opposite his desk, her back ramrod straight. She wasn't here to get cosy and comfortable, she was here to seal this deal.

Clasping her hands in her lap, she fixed him with a businesslike stare.

'Let's get down to it, shall we? You know what I want. You've had time to study the figures in my presentation. What's your answer?'

To her chagrin he grinned, a wide, self-assured grin of a fat cat toying with a baby mouse.

'It's killing you, isn't it?'

In an instant she knew what he was referring to. He used to tease her about being a nosy busybody all the time, so he'd know how much his bombshell was burning her up with curiosity.

As if she'd give him the satisfaction of knowing it.

Keeping her expression carefully blank, she shrugged. 'You're not the only one who's changed. What you've done in the last ten years, why you chose not to tell me the truth out at the farm, that's your business.'

She leaned forward, tapped her presentation folder sitting in prime position in the middle of his desk.

'And this is mine, so let's cut to the chase. Are you willing to make this deal or not?'

'That depends on you.'

He sat, leaned back and clasped his hands behind his head, stretching the fine cotton of his business shirt tight against his chest, drawing her attention, tempting her to stare, to linger, to envision what he looked like without it.

Not that she had to try too hard. She'd had an up close and personal look earlier that day and a glimpse of that entire bronze, hard chest was burned into her memory bank no matter how many times she hit the mental delete button.

She shook her head to clear it. 'Of course I want this deal to happen. It's why I'm here.'

The only reason I'm here, hung unsaid between them as she matched his steady stare, not blinking, not moving a muscle.

To her surprise he broke the deadlock first by reaching for the folder and pushing it towards her with one finger.

'I'm not interested in your money.'

That got her attention.

'Pardon?'

He tapped the folder. 'What your company's offering in here, the remuneration for use of the farm. I'm not interested.'

Her hopes sank faster than her first attempt at rowing on the

Thames as she struggled to come up with a new twist on her pitch, something, anything, to convince him to agree to this deal.

'But I do have something else in mind.'

She didn't like the hint of subterfuge in his smoother-than-caramel tone, the gleam of devilry in his toffee eyes.

'Like what?'

He pushed away from the desk, came around and squatted down next to her, way too close, way too overpowering, way too much.

'I'll agree to your precious deal if you agree to mine.'

His silky smooth tone sent a shiver of dread creeping across the nape of her neck, for she had no doubt whatever demands he made she'd be forced to agree.

Hanging onto her cool by a thread, she tossed her hair over her right shoulder and fixed him with her best intimidating glare.

'Go on, then. State your terms.'

Placing a finger under her chin, he tipped it up, his slight touch sending unexpected heat spiralling through her and slashing a serious hole in her concentration.

'It's quite simple. I hold onto the farm for now, give you complete access for however long you need it, on one condition.'

She leaned forward, drawn towards him against her will, his finger less of a guide than her own stupid attraction when it came to this man.

'Spit it out.'

With his lips a hair's breadth from hers, he murmured, 'You become my wife.'

With their lips so close, so tantalisingly close, and the ever-present heat shimmering between them like an invisible thread binding them despite time apart, it took a few seconds for his words to penetrate.

When they did, she jerked back, shock rendering her speechless.

Her mouth opened, closed, as her mind spun with confusion. She could've sworn he'd just proposed...

'You heard me.'

He straightened, and while half of her wanted to clobber him for the ludicrous statement he'd just made, the other half irrationally missed his proximity.

He perched on the desk, towering over her.

'Marry me. That's my condition.'

'Are you out of your mind?'

She leaped to her feet, stood toe to toe with him. 'What sort of stupid condition is that? Like I'd ever marry you, like I'd agree to—'

'The idea didn't seem so distasteful ten years ago. As I recall, you used to love talking about marrying me.'

Heat flooded her cheeks and she clenched her hands to stop from reaching out and strangling him.

'Come off it, I was young and stupid then.'

'So you're old and wise now?'

His mouth twitched and the itch to strangle him intensified tenfold.

'In that case, you'll see how much sense this makes.'

'None of this makes sense!'

Her temper, which she'd learned to control over the years, exploded like a tinder-dry bush touched by a match. 'You're insane! You've been playing some warped game ever since I saw you this morning and I have no idea why. You pretend you're still working on the farm, you hide your new job from me, then you come out with this ridiculous proposal.'

She paused, dragged in several breaths and released her hands before her nails sliced into her palms.

'I came to you in good faith, to try and put a simple deal forward, and what do I get in return? A bunch of patooey!'

'Patooey?'

This time, his mouth creased into a wide grin and she almost committed murder on the spot.

'Is that London speak for bullsh—'

'It sure is and you're full of it.'

Hands on hips, she leaned into him, shoving her face in his.

'When did you become such a jerk, Mancini?'

While Nick's smile didn't slip, his cool composure cracked a little. The woman he once loved thought he was a jerk and while it shouldn't matter, it did.

But he wouldn't dwell on that. The old Britt was still there, under the fancy business suit and blonde-streaked hair; she'd just shown him with that magnificent temper bursting like a tropical thunderstorm.

The old Britt wouldn't agree to his proposal, while the career-focused woman in sky-high stilettos and a designer suit would if he presented it the right way.

'Consider this a business transaction, a win-win situation for us both. Nothing more, nothing less.'

He saw a flicker of interest flash across her face at his mention of business before her temper flared again.

'You're crazy! Stark raving mad!'

She raked her hands through her immaculately blow-dried hair, sending it into the frizz he remembered. 'What's that expression Papa used to say? *Sei pazzo*, you're crazy, that's what you are.'

His heart griped as it always did at the mention of his father.

'You remember that?'

All the fight drained out of her and she slumped back into the chair, deliciously defeated, and he yearned to sweep her into his arms and show her this deal was the perfect solution for them both.

Raising wide blue eyes to stare at him in capitulation, she nodded.

'I remember a lot of things.'

He waited, captured by the deepening blue, by the emotions shifting like jacaranda blossoms floating on a spring breeze.

He didn't want to feel, certainly didn't want to feel like this, damn it, but when she looked at him with remembrance clouding her eyes and a softening around her lush mouth all he could think about was how incredible she used to feel in his arms.

He didn't want to rehash the past, to taint this deal with emotion, but he couldn't resist asking, 'What do you remember?'

Her tongue darted out to moisten her bottom lip, a simple, unaffected gesture that shot straight to his groin, nothing unaffected about his visceral reaction.

'Like how we used to lie under that jacaranda tree down by the creek and stare up at the clouds and see who could make the craziest shape.'

Her mouth softened some more and he stiffened, shocked by how much he wanted to ravage those lips.

'Like the times you took me into Noosa on the back of your Harley and how we'd choose to picnic down in Noosaville rather than mix with the hobknobs on Hasting Street.'

She gave up moistening her bottom lip in favour of worrying it and he clamped down on a groan.

'Like how you'd look at me with stars in your eyes, as if I was the only woman for you.'

She didn't glance away as he expected her to, didn't push him away when he swept her into his arms and crushed his mouth on hers.

She tasted of lime and sugar, tart and sweet, and he knew she'd been guzzling sugar-cane juice as she used to. She'd been addicted to the stuff back then, just as he'd been addicted to her.

He could never get enough of her and it looked as if nothing had changed as his tongue swept into her mouth, taunting, challenging, savouring her passionate response as she clung to him, her fingers tangling in his buttons as he pulled her flush against him.

This deal was supposed to be purely business but as their kiss deepened to the point of no return he knew he was kidding himself.

What he felt around Britt, how his blood fired when she was in his arms, had nothing to do with business and everything to do with earth-shattering pleasure.

The moment Nick eased off the pressure to kiss his way across her cheek, Brittany froze.

This was where taking a trip down memory lane got her: in the arms of the devil himself.

He'd proposed the most ludicrous deal she'd ever heard in her life and what had she done?

Let him kiss her. Again.

Had responded to him. Again.

She didn't get this, any of it. Business was business but what he'd proposed was…was…well, it was just plain nuts.

Marriage to Nick Mancini in exchange for her dream?

She couldn't entertain the thought for a second, let alone acknowledge the tiny voice that reminded her she'd do anything to achieve her goal.

Well, marriage to Nick didn't fall into the category of anything. It fell into the category of certifiable lunacy.

He set her away from him, his glib smile at odds with the surprising tenderness in his eyes.

'Well, I guess that proves being my wife wouldn't be all bad.'

She summoned her temper, needing it to anchor her threadbare control, that wavered the moment he mentioned the physical benefits to a possible marriage.

'If you think I'd ever agree to your proposal, you're mad.'

He shrugged, stepped away.

'Hey, I'm not the one who wants a promotion. Ball's in your court, Red.'

She hated hearing the nickname only he had ever called her trip from his tongue with familiarity. She hated the blunt truth of his casual statement even more.

She did need this promotion. It was the only way to get closure on a past she'd rather forget.

Studying him through narrowed eyes, she said, 'Not that I'd contemplate your crazy scheme for one second, but if I did, what's in it for you?'

Something furtive, mysterious, shifted behind his steady stare before he blinked, eradicating the enigmatic emotion in an instant.

'It's time I married.'

'Why?'

Why now? Why me? was what she really wanted to ask, but she clamped down on the urge to blurt her questions.

Why he was doing this? Why would he suggest something so outlandish when they shared nothing these days but a residual attraction based on old times' sake?

He shrugged and she hated his nonchalance in the face of something so important. She would've given everything she owned to be married to him once and now he'd reduced it to a cold, calculating business proposition that hurt way more than it should.

'I'm expanding the business, building more hotels in key cities around the world, but overseas investors won't take me seriously because of my age. They see a young, wealthy single guy and immediately think I'm a playboy dabbling in business for fun.'

He rolled his shoulders, tilted his head from side to side to stretch his neck and she stifled the urge to massage it as she used to. He'd always had tense muscles after a hard day's farm work, had relaxed under her soothing hands.

Her palms tingled with the urge to reach out, stroke his

tension away. So she balled her hands into fists and swallowed the unexpected lump in her throat. Damn memories.

He rubbed the back of his neck absent-mindedly, oblivious to her irrational craving to do the same. 'Marriage will give me respectability in their eyes, solidify my entry into wider business circles and open up a whole new investment pool.'

She stared at him, so cool, so confident, admiring the powerful businessman he'd become, lamenting the loss of the bad boy who hadn't given a toss what people thought of him.

'That's it?'

He nodded, showed her his hands palm up as if he wasn't hiding anything.

'That's it.'

'Why me?'

It had been bugging her since he'd first laid out his outlandish proposal, why a guy like him with charm to burn would choose her for his crazy scheme. 'Surely the legendary Nick Mancini would have a bevy of babes around here eager to tie you down?'

His eyes glittered as she inwardly cursed her choice of words and rushed on. 'I mean, why me in particular? What have I got to offer?'

'Do you really want me to answer that?'

Her breath hitched at the clear intent in his loaded stare and she took a step back. 'Yes.'

To her relief, he shrugged, the heat fading from his eyes. 'You're a motivated businesswoman. You wouldn't have flown halfway around the world to make your pitch the best if you weren't. And I need that. Someone with a clear vision in mind, a business goal.'

He pinned her with a firm glare. 'Someone who won't cloud the issue with emotion, which is exactly what would happen if I chose a local wife.'

His hand wavered between them. 'This marriage between

us is a straightforward business proposal, a win-win for us both. What do you think?'

She thought he was mad, but most of all she thought she was a fool for wishing his preposterous proposal held even the slightest hint of emotion she still meant something to him other than as a means to gaining *respectability*.

Summoning what was left of her dignity, she nodded. 'I'll get back to you.'

'You do that.'

His confident grin grated. He knew she was buying time to contemplate his marital equivalent of a pie chart.

With her mind spinning, she stalked across the room, head held high, his soft, taunting chuckles following her out of the door.

CHAPTER FOUR

'SO, THE prodigal daughter returns.'

From the moment Brittany knew she'd be returning home she'd been bracing for this confrontation.

However, no matter that she told herself it was ridiculous, no amount of deep breathing, or steeling her nerves, or trying to remember how far in the past it all was could calm her in any way as she faced her father for the first time in ten years. She could feel her hands shaking.

She paused at the entrance to his apartment, one of the few in the exclusive Jacaranda special accommodation home for the elderly.

Not that Darby Lloyd would ever admit to his seventy-two years. He'd had work done on his face several times, had hair plugs to arrest a threatening bald patch and continued to wear designer clothes better suited to a man half his age.

But pots of money or cosmetic work or fancy clothes couldn't buy health and that was one thing he didn't have these days.

Five years ago, he'd tried to guilt her into quitting her job and returning to look after him as he grew older and more bitter. He'd nearly succeeded. However, some deep part of her had resisted his pressure. He had been a cruel tyrant who'd controlled her life until she'd come into a small inheritance from her mum when she'd turned eighteen and fled as far from him as she could get. She simply couldn't go back to the hell she'd left behind.

In her heart, she desperately wanted to be anywhere but in front of the man who would have ruined her life if she'd let him, but her pride wouldn't let her pay a visit to her hometown and not see him. She was older and stronger— surely she could stand to face him now? She had come here today to prove to herself she'd finally set the past to rest. Working harder, longer, than everyone else might keep the memory demons at bay, but she knew if she stopped, slowed down her frenetic pace, the old fears could come crowding back to fling her right back to the dim, dark place ten years earlier.

And she'd be damned if she let that happen. In a way, she should thank dear old Dad for shaping her into the woman she was today: strong, capable and successful, everything he'd said she'd never be.

But there was more to this visit and she knew it, no matter all her self talk to the contrary.

She was here because of hope.

Hope that he might have changed. Hope that after all this time they might actually have a shot at some semblance of a normal father-daughter relationship.

And if not? Well, she was different now: a woman on top of her career, a woman who depended on no one, a woman a far cry from the victim she'd once been.

She'd vowed back then never to be helpless again, had instigated huge steps to eradicate the confusion and fear, yet as she stood on the threshold to this room trepidation tripped across her skin as the anxiety she'd fought to conquer over the last decade clawed at her belly.

'How are you, Dad?'

'Much the same.'

He limped towards her, waving his cane at a seat for her.
'No thanks to you.'

Taking several deep breaths, she perched on the edge of the
chair, willing the dread to subside, hating the vulnerability
being this close to him elicited.

She needed to do this, needed to see if there was the slightest chance for them before she returned to London.

'You look good.'

He grunted in response, wouldn't meet her gaze, his surly
expression putting a serious dent in her hopes for some kind
of reconciliation.

'This place is lovely.'

Another monosyllabic grunt as his frown deepened and her
patience wore a little thinner.

'Dad, I really think it's time to—'

'What the hell are you doing here?'

His snarl caught her off guard despite his churlishness, yet
it wasn't his response that saddened her as much as the
contempt in his truculent glare.

She'd been a fool to hope for anything other than what she
got: more of the same from a boorish man who didn't give a
hoot about her.

'I'm here on business.'

He showed no interest, seemed bored more than anything
else. Faced with his silence she could not help asking him:

'Don't you want to know how I am? What I've been doing?
What I've achieved?'

His withering stare clued her into his response before he
spoke.

'I don't give a damn any more.'

Pain sliced her heart in two, the old familiar questions re-
verberating through her head: *What did I do wrong? Why did
you stop loving me? Could I have done anything differently?*

But she wasn't the same scared teenager any more.

She had her career skyrocketing all the way to the top and she'd be damned if she sat here and took any of his crap.

Resisting the urge to jab her finger at him to ram home her point, she sat back, folded her arms and looked him straight in the eye.

'Maybe you should give a damn. That way, you'd know I'm a senior executive at a top London ad firm, that I'm good at what I do and I've done it all on my own, no thanks to you.'

She'd come here with some semblance of the idealistic girl she'd once been, but that girl vanished beneath his lack of caring and she wanted to rub his nose in her independence, in her success, in the proof she'd survived despite what he'd put her through.

If she'd thought her outburst would gain a reaction, gain recognition for her achievements, she should've known better.

He glowered, drew himself up, resembling the towering giant of a man she remembered as he rammed his cane against the floor.

'You're a fool if you think I care about any of that.'

Her heart ached as she stared at the man who was her father biologically but didn't know the meaning of the word.

She could rant and rave and fling past hurts or present triumphs in his face but what would be the point? Darby listened to no one but himself, which was why he now found himself in this place. No amount of money on offer had induced anyone locally to play nursemaid and she couldn't blame them.

Slinging her bag higher on her shoulder, she kept her face devoid of pity for the father she'd never had.

'Sorry you feel that way. I thought…'

What? That the old despot might've changed, might've mellowed with time and illness? Not likely. If anything, his belligerence had worsened and she'd been crazy to come here, setting the past to rest while hoping for a miracle.

'Thought what? I'd welcome you with open arms after all this time?'

He snorted, waved his good hand towards the door. 'Just leave the way you came in.'

She'd cried rivers of wasted tears when she was a teenager for all this man had put her through and there was no way she'd stand here now and allow him to reduce her to tears again.

With a shake of her head, she turned away, ready to walk out and never look back.

'That's it, run away again. Though this time, you won't have a penny of mine to cushion you when you fall.'

Icy foreboding trickled down her spine as she slowly swung back to face him.

'What did you just say?'

His malevolent grin raised goose bumps on her skin. 'You heard. That money from your mother? It was a crock. She never left you a cent. That was my money you squandered on your little trip, my money that made sure you didn't end up in the gutter.'

She staggered, leaned against the doorway for support, her gut twisting with the painful truth.

'So, daughter dearest, looks like you owe me after all.'

With his words ringing in her ears, she stumbled from the apartment, from the accommodation and made it to her car before she collapsed, slumping over the steering wheel.

She'd thought she'd escaped his stranglehold ten years earlier, had fought hard for her independence, had found safety and confidence in her career.

She'd been wrong.

Right then, she vowed to do whatever it took to pay off her debt.

You owe me...

With the hateful truth ringing in her ears, her head snapped up as she straightened, knowing what she had to do.

There was only one thing that would clear a debt of that magnitude and, right now, gaining her promotion was a necessity.

In choosing between owing her dad a huge amount of money and agreeing to Nick's outlandish proposal, marrying Nick would be the lesser of two evils.

She'd come.

Nick squinted at Brittany between the spokes of his Harley, trying to read her expression and coming up empty.

She'd left a message for him at the hotel desk requesting a meeting and he had suggested to meet at the farm, hoping that the memories might throw her off balance—make her vulnerable, more easily manipulated. He hadn't anticipated that those very same memories might unsettle him as well, but with Britt standing there, dressed in a short white skirt and pink vest-top, gnawing at her full bottom lip, an action he remembered all too well, attending to his bike was the last thing on his mind.

He waited for her to speak, continued polishing the chrome, an action he found soothing. He rarely got time to lavish on his bike these days and this was the first opportunity he'd had to work on his baby in months.

Even with her forget-me-not eyes clouded with worry, tendrils of hair escaping her ponytail and draping her face in golden copper and that worried action which drew attention to her lush mouth like it always had, she looked incredible, like his greatest fantasy come to life.

Which she was, not that he'd ever told her. He'd had his chance ten years earlier and she'd made it more than clear what she'd thought of his rebuff back then.

'You blow this chance, Mancini, you'll never get another one. This is it, you and me, together. So what will it be?'

His answer had been pretty clear. He'd given her one last kiss, a bruising, harsh kiss to say goodbye to the best thing that could've happened to him, pushed her away and said, 'There is no us, Red. And there never will be.'

She hadn't cried and he'd admired her for it. She hadn't clung or tried to change his mind. She'd sent him a pitying look, shook her long red mane, held her head high and walked out on him, leaving him with an ache in the vicinity of his heart. An ache that had returned tenfold despite all his self talk what they'd shared back then was nothing more than a teenage fling.

Slamming a door on pointless memories, he stood, tucked the polishing cloth in his back pocket and leaned against the bike.

'You made it.'

For a second, he wished he hadn't sounded so flippant as her eyes clouded with wariness.

'Yeah, thanks for agreeing to meet me.'

The hint of vulnerability in her voice, in her expression, stunned him. The Brittany Lloyd he knew would never show weakness in front of anybody, least of all him.

'Let's pull up a seat.' He pointed to the outer perimeter of the machinery shed, where a few old-fashioned plastic garden chairs lay scattered. 'Have you given any more thought to my proposal?'

Stupid question. As if she would've thought of anything else since she'd stormed out of his office yesterday.

She ignored his question and said, 'I want to talk about my father.'

No way.

If there was one topic of conversation off-limits, that was it.

Darby Lloyd was an out and out bastard. He'd controlled everything and everyone in this district, had set out to ruin Papa. Until Nick had given him what he wanted.

Rubbing the back of his neck, he said, 'I don't have much to say on that topic.'

'Not many people do. But I want to know something. Did

he ever approach you about me back when we were dating? Did he try to interfere?'

His blood chilled. There was no way he'd ever tell her the truth about her father. Besides, it wasn't as if Darby were the cause of their break-up. It'd been much easier to blame their disintegrated relationship on her wanting to escape Jacaranda for the bright lights of a big city. That way, he could live with himself and what he'd done.

To help justify their break-up he'd told himself women were fickle. His aunt had run off to Melbourne with a salesman, his godmother had absconded with the butcher to Bunbury, his mum had abandoned her family and Britt had followed suit, hightailing it to London as soon as she hit eighteen.

Britt might have invited him along for the ride but he'd known that was due to the teenage fantasy she'd built in her head, the one where she saw him as some fancy Prince Charming riding his white horse to save her.

The problem with fantasies was they weren't true and he'd been forced to burst her bubble before he did something silly—such as trust her as he'd trusted his mother.

'What did he do? Tell me.'

She clicked her fingers in front of his face and as he looked into her luminous blue eyes a small part of him wished he'd indulged her fantasy.

Where would they be today if he had? Happily married with a brood of ruffians? Sharing confidences and dreams? Spending every night wrapped in each other's arms, recreating the magic, the passion, that haunted him to this day? He could've had one hell of a life.

But he'd made his choices, his sacrifices, and, considering the successful hotelier he'd become, life wasn't all bad.

'Just thinking of the good old days,' he said, trying to distract her. He didn't want to talk about her father, not now, not ever.

'Good old days?'

She gaped at him and he clamped down on a grin. 'Which ones? The ones where you tied my plaits to the bus seat, or the ones where you plucked my lunch right out of my hands, or the ones where you threw my pet rock collection into the river?'

He smiled at the memories, remembering how he'd used to tease her mercilessly and how she'd given as good as she'd got. She'd been a little firebrand back then, her red hair a definite symbol of a quick-fire temper. And a symbol of a simmering passion he'd been lucky enough to unleash.

Man, had she pushed his buttons back then and he hoped to God he'd grown out of it, whatever *it* was.

He didn't have time for emotions in this marriage. It was business, pure and simple. He had more important matters to consider, such as building his profile with investors, expanding into new cities and upping profit margins.

'You loved every minute of it. Remember that time I put a toad in your bag?'

She rolled her eyes, a smile twitching at the corners of her glossed lips. 'Oh yeah, I really loved that. Not!'

'How about the garlic I rubbed into your Spandau Ballet T-shirt?'

Her lips twitched more. 'You were a jerk.'

'What about the shed incident?'

'Which one?'

Her lips curved into a small, secretive smile and he clenched his hands into fists and thrust them into his pockets to prevent them reaching for her.

'The time you had me shovelling manure or the time you opened your mouth and poured the verbal variety on me so I'd fall into your arms?'

'Ouch!' He clutched at his heart. 'You haven't changed a bit, Red. That hurt.'

'And you haven't changed a bit either, still shovelling it in the hope to distract me. Now, can we get back to the topic of my father?'

She was onto him. Always had been, seeing right through his tough-guy act, reducing him to a love-struck schmuck around her.

Correction, lust-struck schmuck.

Big difference there. He'd never loved Brittany. Liked her, lusted after her but he'd never dared love her.

He didn't do love.

Love equalled loss and loneliness and pain, emotions he could do without.

Folding his arms, he leaned back in the rickety chair. If he couldn't deflect her attention, he'd have to give her some snippet of the truth to placate her before they tackled more important matters, like the question of their impending nuptials.

'You know how much your dad hated any guy who came near you. Why dredge all this up now?'

She gnawed at her bottom lip, fiddled with the edge of her short skirt. He'd never seen her this nervous before.

Well, maybe on one other occasion, the night she'd asked him to go away with her, the night he'd made the final break.

Until yesterday, he'd convinced himself he'd made the right decision. Women were unpredictable, erratic creatures who couldn't be depended on. Then Brittany Lloyd walked back into his life, making him re-evaluate his choice and think a whole lot of 'what-ifs'.

What if he'd gone away with her?

What if they'd made a life together?

What if they fell in love and lived happily ever after?

Yeah, like happy-ever-afters ever happened in the real world.

'Because I visited him yesterday.' She raised stricken eyes to his and it took every ounce of will power not to reach out, bundle her into his arms and comfort her. 'He hasn't changed a bit.'

He swallowed the bitterness that rose at the thought of Darby Lloyd and his far-reaching tentacles poisoning everything and everyone around him, including this remarkably special woman.

He hadn't blamed her for running away. He'd wondered what took her so long.

Unable to resist, he reached out and took hold of her hand, surprised and more than a little grateful when she let him. 'Want to know what I think?'

She nodded, her eyes wide with pain.

'You've moved on. From what you've told me, you're a successful businesswoman with one hell of a career so don't let the past suck you back in.'

He squeezed her hand, trailed his thumb across the back of it. 'It's not worth it.'

Brittany couldn't meet his gaze; it was far too kind. Far too full of memories.

'Thanks,' she muttered, and made an angry swipe at her eyes, dashing away the tears pooled there. She'd done nothing but make a fool of herself since she'd arrived in Jacaranda: making assumptions about Nick, letting him kiss her, hoping her father had changed. She didn't need to start blubbering like a two-year-old to top it off.

Teasing Nick she could handle. Compassionate Nick, holding her hand and staring at her with unquestionable warmth in his eyes, had the potential to undo her completely.

'Hey, don't cry.'

He leaned over and brushed away the tears that had spilled over and run down her cheeks.

Great. Just her luck she hadn't worn waterproof mascara today.

'Jet lag catching up with me,' she muttered, blinking rapidly only to find a veritable flood seeping out of her eyes.

'Come here, you.'

Before she could protest, Nick hauled her into his arms and cradled her close, smoothing her hair, making small crooning noises. Being enveloped in his strong arms, her face pressed against hard chest wall, surrounded by his familiar scent of sugar and spice and all things nice, should've soothed her.

It didn't. Being held by Nick dammed her tears but it resurrected a host of feelings that had nothing to do with comfort.

Desire seeped through her body as he continued stroking her hair, rendering her powerless to move. She couldn't have pulled away if she wanted to. And, God help her, she didn't want to.

She inhaled deeply, allowing the heady combination of sugar-cane sweetness, metal polish and tropical sunshine to flood her lungs, enjoying the momentary lapse in reason as she wished he could hold her like this for ever.

Sliding her arms around his waist, she allowed her hands the luxury of smoothing across hard muscle, revelling in the heat radiating through his cotton T-shirt.

Closing her eyes, she sighed, knowing there was no place in the world she'd rather be than right here.

London was her life now, the vibrant city a part of her new persona but even with her career shooting into the stratosphere, at times like this, in the warm embrace of an incredible man, it wasn't enough.

She'd tried to forget Nick, had rarely succeeded: wondering what he was doing, who he was doing it with, where they would be if he'd said yes to her all those years ago.

'You okay now?'

He pulled back with such swiftness she almost fell off her chair.

'Yeah, thanks.'

She scanned his face for an indication of what he was thinking, but true to form the Mancini mask had slipped into place, leaving her wondering what was going on behind those enigmatic dark eyes. She'd seen it their last night together ten years ago, the night he'd broken her heart.

'We have other business to discuss.'

Her heart sank.

For those all too brief moments when he'd held her, she'd forgotten the reason she'd requested this meeting. But the thought of her father, as poisonous as a puffer fish, leaped to mind and she knew she had to do this.

It was the only way.

She needed this promotion now more than ever, needed the money to clear a debt she'd never known existed and the sooner that was done, the better. Then she'd finally be free.

'You're right, we do need to talk.'

She twisted a strand of hair around her finger, a habit she'd long conquered, before belatedly releasing it. What was it about this guy that obliterated the last ten years as if they'd never happened and thrust her back to a time she'd rather forget?

'I have an answer to your proposal.'

'And?'

He propped against the bike, looking every bit the bad boy rebel he'd once been: dark, devastating, delicious.

She swallowed, her throat clenching with how much she still wanted him after all this time.

He might've proposed a marriage for business purposes but deep down she knew there wasn't a chance in hell she'd be able to keep her hands off him. And considering he'd kissed her, twice, she had an inkling the feeling was mutual.

So where did that leave them? What would the boundaries of their marriage be? Monogamous? Casual?

He straightened, stepped closer to her.

'Stop over-analysing this. Give me your answer and we'll go from there.'

With her heart pounding and heat from his proximity prickling her skin, she wrenched her gaze from his chest within tantalising touching distance and slowly raised it until wavering blue locked with questioning brown.

Her voice barely above a whisper, she nodded.

'My answer is yes.'

CHAPTER FIVE

NICK snuck in the side entrance of the conference room, not wanting to intrude but driven by curiosity.

Since Britt had agreed to his proposal, she'd morphed into a businesswoman dervish, throwing herself into work at a speed that made him, a confirmed workaholic, seem like a snail.

She'd commandeered the business centre of the hotel, had turned this room into a hive of activity.

In less than a day.

He shook his head, beyond impressed at her work ethic. He'd never seen her like this: focused, determined, driven, issuing orders and delegating to the team she'd assembled in record time.

Watching her in a power suit the colour of ripe plums, her hair twisted in a fancy topknot and her brow creased in concentration while she tapped on a keyboard with one hand and shuffled documents with the other, he understood why she'd said yes to his proposal.

Her job meant everything to her and, while he empathised with her ambition, he couldn't help but wish some of her agreement stemmed from the sexual tension strumming between them.

A surge of heat at the memory of kissing her had him sliding a finger between his neck and suddenly too tight collar.

Their marriage might be motivated by business, but who said they couldn't have a real honeymoon?

Her head snapped up and their gazes locked, as if he'd inadvertently telepathised his thoughts and he grinned, sent her a half-salute, not surprised when she frowned and gestured towards the stack of paperwork in front of her.

She didn't want him here.

His cue to saunter across the room and drop into the vacant chair next to her.

'How's it going?'

Frowning, she barely glanced at him. 'Busy.'

'So I see.'

'Don't you have work of your own to do?'

Leaning back, he linked his fingers and stretched. 'I'm taking a break.'

He smothered an outright laugh as she glared. 'Anything I can do to help?'

'No, all under control.'

Her laptop screen flickered and she swore, making a mockery of her previous statement.

'I've got the latest technology in my office if you need it.'

'I said I was fine,' she snapped, rubbing the bridge of her nose before mustering an apologetic smile. 'Sorry. I'm used to having my team around me in London. It's harder trying to get a cohesive unit together so quickly here.'

'Why the rush?'

He knew she'd see right through his innocuous question, knew she'd understand what he was really asking was 'how long are you sticking around?'

With her gaze firmly fixed on her laptop screen, she said, 'Deadlines. I'm sure you understand.'

Placing a hand on her arm, he leaned across to murmur in her ear. 'How long, Red?'

She stared at his hand as if it were a tiger snake before finally raising her eyes to his.

'I don't know. This pitch is big. Huge. The MD didn't set an exact timeline but he knows I'm a fast worker. As long as I deliver, it's up to me.'

He wanted to push the issue, wanted to discuss how long they'd have to make this marriage as real as it could get, but now wasn't the time or place.

Squeezing her arm, he released her and glanced at his watch. 'I do have an appointment, but we should get together later to discuss our *other business*.'

Her eyes widened as the pen in her right hand started rapping a frenetic rhythm against the Manila folder in front of her.

Amazing how the mention of their pending marriage could change her from uber-cool career-woman to nervous Nelly.

'I'm not sure how long I'll be here. I have loads to do, then I need to head out to the farm—'

'Perfect. We can discuss our plans over dinner.'

She opened her mouth to refuse and he raised an eyebrow, daring her to disagree.

'Not having second thoughts, are you? Because if you are, I might have to expedite the sale of the farm and—'

'Fine, I'll see you there.'

The coolness in her tone belied the angry flush creeping up her neck as he marvelled again at how damn important this promotion must be for her to go through with this.

Marrying for convenience occurred a fair bit in the business world, but never in his wildest dreams had he thought he'd do it, let alone to the only woman he would've ever contemplated walking down the aisle with once upon a time.

'Glad that's settled.'

He stood, looked down at her elaborate hairdo, his fingers itching to tug the pins out and send the whole thing tumbling around her shoulders.

As if sensing his thoughts again, she tilted back on the chair, glared at him. 'Was there anything else, because you're hovering?'

With a smile designed to provoke a response, he ducked down to murmur in her ear. 'I'll cook, but I hope you remember how much I love dessert.'

As the pen picked up tempo again he chuckled, snatched a hairpin and laid it on the stack of paperwork in front of her, before heading for the door.

'I brought dessert.'

Brittany held out the store-bought lemon meringue pie, wishing Nick would take the damn thing before it tumbled from her shaking hands.

This dinner was supposed to set her mind at rest, a pre-wedding get-together to discuss plans and take the edge off her nerves.

So far, it wasn't working.

'Thanks, looks delicious.'

His gaze flicked over her, appreciation lighting his eyes, and she had no doubt he wasn't talking about the pie.

She'd spent an hour deciding what to wear, aiming for casual yet wanting to make him look twice. After five changes she'd finally decided on caramel suede trousers sitting low on her hips and a chocolate rib top that fitted like a second skin. The warm tones highlighted her hair and skin to perfection, or so some stylist had told her at Harrods.

In London, she'd taken her appearance for granted, spending a small fortune on clothes and accessories to fit the image of a top marketing consultant. She dressed to impress, was used to it. That was her excuse for wanting to look her best tonight. Yeah, right.

'What's for dinner?'

She headed for the stove in an attempt to escape Nick's intense stare.

'Antipasto for starters, home-made ravioli filled with asparagus and leeks, smothered in a four-cheese herb sauce for main.'

He picked up a ladle, lifted a pot lid and stirred, the delicious aroma of melted cheese and garlic filling the kitchen and making her mouth water.

'You make your own pasta?'

She raised an eyebrow, beyond impressed. How did the guy find time to run a hotel, do stuff around the farm and be a whiz in the kitchen?

He cocked a hip and shrugged, deliciously smug and modest at the same time.

'What can I say? I'm a regular Neil Perry.'

'Who?'

'Australia's equivalent to Jamie Oliver,' he said, sprinkling fresh chopped parsley into the pot, sending her a cheeky grin that notched up the heat in the kitchen.

Either that or she was taking a lot longer to acclimatise to the Jacaranda humidity than expected.

'I'm impressed. Is there anything you can't do?'

'No, though I guess I'm better at some things than others.'

He winked and turned back to the stove, his attention riveted to the pot bubbling away while an embarrassing blush crept into her cheeks.

Oh, yeah, she remembered exactly how good he was at some things, which was why she grabbed the cutlery off the sideboard, trying to remember the difference between left and right as she struggled to place knives, forks and spoons in their right place.

She'd been insane to agree to his marriage proposal, absolutely stark, raving mad to think she could remain business-like for the length of their marriage—yet another thing they had to decide tonight. For she was in little doubt this platonic union would have a time limit.

He'd asked as much earlier and she'd had no idea how to respond, didn't want to think beyond this pitch and what she had to do to secure her promotion.

Marriage to Nick, a business deal. And business deals had set time frames, both parties aware of how long the proposed business would take right from the start.

So why the sudden pang in the vicinity of her heart?

Once the table was set, she picked up the pasta bowls and took them to the stove.

'We've got a lot to talk about tonight.'

He held up a hand. 'Not on an empty stomach. Let's eat first.'

'Fine with me.'

But it wasn't fine, none of this was, and while they made polite small talk over his fabulous pasta she couldn't forget the real reason she was here: to set the boundaries of their marriage.

An event she'd dreamed of ten years ago, had planned in her head to the nth degree: strolling towards her incredible groom under the shade of their favourite jacaranda tree down by the river, him in a casual suit with his shirt collar open, the wind ruffling his too-long-to-be-neat hair, her in a flowing ivory silk minidress made for strolling down by the river after she'd married the man of her dreams.

Somehow, the quick, impersonal ceremony in front of a minister they would now go through didn't have the same ring to it.

There went her heart again, squeezing tight, hurting enough to show, no matter how much she pretended this was all business, she knew, deep down, she was selling her soul.

Nick tried not to stare at Brittany, he really did, but it was like trying not to look at the sun glistening on Jacaranda River first thing in the morning or the moon rising over a glittering Noosa at night.

Perfectly natural occurrences where a person's gaze was riveted by beauty, unable to do otherwise and that was exactly how he felt now, taking in her slight frown, pursed lips and thoughtful expression as she tapped a pen against the pad in her hands.

'We're forgetting something,' she said, screwing her eyes up as if trying to see the missing info.

From where he sat, the only thing forgotten was how damn good it felt to be with her like this.

'Want me to take a look?'

'Uh-huh,' she answered absent-mindedly, not looking up from the pad. 'I was sure we'd covered everything but...'

He perched on the couch next to her, grateful for the opportunity to get closer to the woman who was driving him slowly insane with every flutter of her mascaraed eyelashes, with every teasing smile.

Dinner had been a quiet affair and her genuine appreciation for his culinary skills made him feel like a god, yet the underlying tension with every glance, every smile, stretched taut between them.

While she looked amazing tonight, her fancy top and figure-hugging trousers outlining her body to perfection, a body that beckoned him to trace its contours, to feel every gorgeous line, it was more than that.

They'd slipped back into the comfortable camaraderie they used to share and he was thrilled. While he had no illusions about this marriage being anything other than what it was— a convenient business arrangement—it would be so much easier to be friends.

Or more than friends, if he was lucky. He wanted her just as badly now as he ever had, the driving hunger startling and ferocious and capable of sending him bonkers.

'Are you going to help me or just sit there with that goofy look on your face?'

She waved the pen under his nose and he managed a rueful grin. He'd settle for goofy when, the way his thoughts had been heading, she would've been more accurate in describing him as drooling.

'Let me take a look.'

He leaned towards her, a swift stab of longing shooting straight to his groin as a waft of her vanilla perfume hit him.

Vanilla: warm, sweet, tempting.

Exactly how he saw her. The same tantalising scent she'd worn that fateful night ten years ago, the night he'd told her there would never be anything between them.

He just wished he had the same self-control now, but with her inches away, looking like his living, breathing fantasy, a guy could only take so much.

'This list has stuff for you to do and the stuff I can help with.'

She tapped her pen against the paper in a sharp staccato sound, an action fast becoming a nervous habit, and he struggled to focus on her writing, more intrigued by the streaks of blonde through her copper hair and the way they highlighted her beautiful face.

'What's missing?'

'This.'

He tipped her chin up, drinking in her slightly flushed cheeks, her sparkling blue eyes, her glossed lips. Man, she was a stunner, and as a spark of desire flared in her eyes he knew this time he wouldn't be satisfied with a few kisses.

As he moved towards her she stiffened and pulled away.

'We need to concentrate. The sooner we get married, the sooner I can really get started on my work around here and the sooner I get my promotion. Capish?'

She sent him a nervous smile before waving the pad in his

face and, though he'd love nothing better than to see if her desire matched his, he relented.

The mention of her promotion did it. She was doing this for her career, as he was, with no place for emotions to cloud the issue.

Scanning the extensive list she'd made, he pointed to the last few asterisks.

'The licence, the legalities, all taken care of.'

When she quirked an eyebrow, he shrugged. 'Things get done when you have money.'

A shadow passed over her face and he silently cursed his choice of words. If anyone knew the cause and effect of money, she did. Her father threw enough of the green stuff around to buy whatever and whoever he wanted.

He should know.

'So the venue's all taken care of?'

For the first time since she'd arrived tonight, his confidence wavered.

'I thought the hotel garden would be a good spot? Beneath that poinciana tree near the pool?'

It was a perfect spot for a wedding, or so he'd been told by many guests: the towering umbrella-shaped tree laden with bright red flowers, Noosa beach in the background, clear blue ocean as far as the eye could see.

Britt had made him all too aware this marriage was a business merger, nothing more, yet he remembered how sentimental she'd get over the slightest thing and, while she appeared aloof with the planning, he'd bet his last dollar she'd want something a tad special.

'That's fine.'

Her pen picked up tempo as she focused on the list, obviously eager to get this over and done with so she could escape. Accepting this marriage was business was one thing, having to pretend to like it another.

Why did that rankle so much? It wasn't as if this were remotely romantic yet somehow, ever since she'd returned—and returned his kisses—he'd been having strange pains in his chest, the type of pain he used to have when she was around all those years ago.

She intrigued him, infuriated him, inflamed him and, though he tried to dismiss this marriage as a means to a goal, deep down he knew better.

He'd always wanted a family, the type of family he'd never had, and the only woman he'd ever let get close was sitting less than a foot away with fiddling fingers and a wary gleam in her blue eyes.

'Anything else?'

'What about a notice in the newspaper for an authentic touch?'

'That's it.' She jotted it down. 'I'd call you a genius but it'd just go to your head.'

'Try me.'

He leaned towards her with the sole intention of brushing a stray tendril of hair from her forehead. He never got the chance as their gazes locked for a heated moment before she leaped off the couch.

'Right, we're all done here. Thanks for dinner, it was great.' She shoved the notebook into her bag, slung it over her shoulder. 'I'm pretty tired, so I'll head off now. Big day Friday.'

With an overly bright smile, she practically ran around the room. 'I'll get a copy of this list to you tomorrow. We don't have much time to get everything organised, so the sooner we get it done, the better. I'll—'

'Red?'

'Yeah?'

She paused mid-flight and took a deep breath, the simple action drawing his attention to her breasts and the way they filled out her ribbed top.

'For a city girl, you're sure behaving like a country virgin.'

He expected a host of retorts, or at least one decent smart-ass remark.

Instead, she glared at him, flushed a deep crimson and bolted out of the door.

Brittany wriggled her toes in her favourite Garfield slippers, pulled her fluffy tangerine robe tighter and cradled a hot chocolate while scanning her emails.

Not that she needed the extra calories after the mountain of food she'd consumed at Nick's, but chocolate didn't count, especially of the liquid variety. Besides, the way she was feeling right now, she needed comfort food, and this was it.

Nick had been right, damn him.

She *had* behaved like a country virgin, the exact way she used to act around him ten years earlier, jumping like a cane toad whenever he glanced her way; which had been often, though that hadn't been the hard part.

The hard part had come when he'd looked at her as if he wanted to gobble her up and come back for more. Several times.

As for that almost-kiss…yikes! She'd deflected it with some pathetic line about needing to concentrate, but he hadn't been fooled. She'd seen it by the knowing glint in his toffee eyes, by the smirk that had played around his kissable lips. And they were definitely kissable.

She'd wanted that kiss so badly she'd almost tasted it yet had done the smart thing and fobbed him off.

Smart for whom?

For both of them. She wasn't interested in making this marriage real. She had a successful career waiting for her in London, a fabulous promotion, good friends, a great apartment. Everything a girl could want.

But what if she wanted more?

If she did, Nick Mancini sure wasn't the guy to give it to her. His life was poles apart from hers.

His business was here, hers was in London.

His heritage was here, she'd always craved to escape family here.

He didn't want a real marriage, a small part of her did.

Huh?

Where had that last bit come from?

Sighing, she took a comforting sip of the creamy hot chocolate, savouring the mini marshmallows melting on her tongue.

Unfortunately, as fabulous as her life in London was, there was one thing lacking and that was a real, steady relationship. Not some casual fling, not some short-term dating and not some modern equivalent of 'being involved'—meeting once a week for a regular meal and sex. She'd tried these options and found them infinitely depressing.

No man had come close to matching what she'd felt for Nick, had once had with Nick.

And therein lay her problem.

'Just great,' she muttered, hitting the delete key on several joke emails and wishing she could erase her feelings for Nick as easily.

She'd been back a few days and had already reverted to her old ways: thinking about him constantly, wondering what he thought of her, hoping he felt half of what she did.

Pathetic.

The last email in her inbox effectively distracted her from the Nick problem. Her boss had given her leeway to complete this job, so why send her an email with 'Tight Timeline' in the subject header?

Clicking on the email, she quickly scanned the contents.

TO: BrittanyLloyd@Sell.London.com

FROM: DavidWaterson@Sell.London.com

SUBJECT: Tight Timeline
Hi Brittany,

How's my number one marketing guru enjoying her trip Down Under? Working hard, I hope.

I know we left your timeline fairly open for this pitch, but there's a change in plans.

Looks like Sell is expanding the NY office sooner than we thought and they want me to head it up ASAP, which means my job here needs to be filled within three months.

To be fair to all prospective candidates, we'd need your pitch presented in eight weeks.

Hope this is viable. If not, contact me.

We're expecting big things from you, don't let us down.

David

Brittany rubbed a weary hand across her eyes and quickly reread the email.

Eight weeks.

Two brief months to collate information, take pictures and perfect her pitch. Oh, and throw in a snap wedding.

What was she thinking?

But if the wedding didn't happen, she wouldn't have access to the farm, and no access meant no chance at the promotion anyway.

Her hands were tied. So why did it feel as if her insides were following suit?

Off the record, David had virtually assured her the MD role if she presented a killer pitch. She should be doing cartwheels.

Instead, the longer she stared at her boss's email, the more aware she became of exactly how far away London was from Noosa…and her soon-to-be husband who resided there.

CHAPTER SIX

'THIS place has changed so much.'

Brittany's head swivelled from side to side as she strolled up Hastings Street, Noosa's main thoroughfare, with Nick.

'Boutiques, cafés, restaurants, five-star hotels. We almost rival London in the trendy stakes, huh?'

'Almost.'

London had a vibe all of its own and she loved it, and coming home to find Noosa had turned hip and cosmopolitan was a nice surprise.

Nick laid a hand on her arm and she stopped, more startled by his touch than the mini-city's transformation. 'There is one thing we didn't discuss the other night.'

Just one? She could think of several, including how platonic this marriage would be, where they would live, how long they'd keep up the pretence. And that was just for starters.

'What's that?'

'How long you're sticking around for.'

She had to tell him the truth, had to tell him they had eight weeks to make it look as if they had a pretend marriage for real.

Shrugging, she pointed to the tapas bar they'd stopped outside.

'All depends on how long the job takes. Fancy a snack? I'm starving.'

'Okay.'

He led her into the bar, to a cosy table in the furthest corner, and ordered for them before turning that penetrating dark gaze back on her.

'So are we talking two months? Four? Longer?'

'You're really hung up on this timeline thing, aren't you?'

He raised an eyebrow. 'I wouldn't call it a hang-up. An honest answer will do.'

Hating the little white lie she had to tell, she said, 'As long as it takes. I have the workers in place, so once we're married I can really get stuck in.'

She picked at an olive from a tray that had been placed in front of them. 'I guess you want to know what happens after I'm done.'

To her surprise, he shook his head. 'Not really. I'm more concerned with the here and now, and solidifying my reputation with investors.'

She could leave well enough alone. In fact, she'd rather be discussing anything than their cold, calculating marriage scheduled for the morning. But if she left in two months as planned, where would that leave Nick and his precious reputation?

'So when I leave...'

She trailed off, not wanting to voice her doubts out loud. The way she saw it, she was getting the better end of this deal: full access to the farm to nail her promotion then she walked, back to her old life, leaving Nick to fend off curiosity about why his marriage fell apart so quickly and the possible financial fallout from his investors.

'When you leave, I act like nothing is wrong. We'll have a modern marriage, where we spend several months of the year together and have highly successful careers on different continents. Business people understand that.'

'But—'

'It's nobody's concern but ours,' he said, his tone cool and confident, at odds with the banked heat in his enigmatic gaze. 'This is going to work. Trust me.'

He placed a hand over hers before she could blink and rather than pulling away, the sane thing to do, she turned hers over and curled her fingers through his.

With a squeeze, he smiled and her heart flip-flopped in predictable fashion.

'That's my girl. So, you ready for tomorrow?'

'Ready as I'll ever be.'

She'd found a dress in a high-end boutique, shoes to match and had booked a hairdresser appointment.

Did a simple outfit constitute ready? A smart up-do? In reality, she'd never be ready to walk down the aisle with the only guy she'd ever really loved, knowing their marriage was fake.

'About the honeymoon…'

She snapped her gaze to his, not liking the naughty twinkle in his one little bit. 'A honeymoon isn't part of the deal.'

She all but yanked her hand out of his on the pretext of reaching for her water glass. He shrugged, a roguish smile playing about his mouth, and in that moment she wished she could take it back.

She'd always been a sucker for that smile, from the first moment he'd squatted to pick up her books strewn in the dirt when she'd tumbled off the bus the day they'd met.

He'd smiled his way into her life, her heart, and she'd be damned if she sat here and let him do it all over again.

'Okay, no honeymoon.'

'Good.'

She folded her arms, glared at him. With little effect if his growing grin was any indication.

'But we do need to have a wedding night.'

'No way—'

'This marriage has to look real. I'm a prominent business-man in the area and if we don't go away, we'd have to do something special for our wedding night, otherwise people would talk.'

He had a point, damn him.

No biggie. They could share a room; didn't mean they'd have to do anything in it.

'Fine,' she gritted out, her admission as painful as the time she'd had to admit she'd sent him that secret admirer Valentine's card in eighth grade.

Leaning forward, he whispered in her ear. 'You won't be disappointed.'

Hating the surge of lust that made her knees shake beneath the table, she managed a mute nod while sending a silent prayer heavenward for strength.

She had a feeling she'd need it to resist what the reformed bad boy had in mind come tomorrow.

Brittany's hand shook as she waved the mascara wand over her lashes and she blinked several times, grateful she'd chosen the waterproof kind.

She'd already been near tears twice, first when she'd opened the door to a gorgeous bouquet of frangipanis and then when she'd carefully hung her wedding dress encased in plastic on the back of the door.

Nick had sent the flowers. His note had been brief.

For my bride
Nick, x

While the flowers were breathtaking, that one little x had her clutching them and burying her nose in their heady fragrance, her eyes filling to the brim.

She wanted his kisses, wanted him, and, no matter how many times she told herself this wedding was a necessity to be free of her past, she knew when she walked up the aisle shortly she'd want him more than ever.

As for her dress…

She'd wanted to buy something understated, practical, a dress she could wear again, for why spend money on a real dress when this marriage would be far from real?

That was before she laid eyes on the strapless, sweetheart gown in ruched ivory silk chiffon and her neglected romantic soul demanded she buy it.

And she had, for when she touched the dress she imagined magic.

A magical marriage filled with light and laughter and love.

A magical mirage of a handsome groom with stars in his eyes and a bride who believed in the happily ever after she'd always dreamed about.

A magical mystery, that despite their motivations for this marriage they were embarking on something truly wonderful today.

Taking one last look in the mirror, satisfied she hadn't streaked her make-up in a fit of misplaced sentimentality, she shook her head.

Magic wasn't real and she was foolish to dream of anything other than what this marriage was: a business arrangement.

She slipped off her robe and padded across the room to the wardrobe, her fingers trembling as she slid the zip open on the dress's carrier bag.

Every metallic slide, every crinkle of the thick plastic, every rustle of silk chiffon brought her closer to her wedding and her tummy twisted as she reverently lifted the dress out.

Emotion clogged her throat and she swallowed several times as the soft flowing skirt cascaded to the floor in a silken ripple.

The dress was a dream, and her breath whooshed out as she steeled her nerve and slowly, carefully stepped into it, wishing she could channel some of that magic.

Closing her eyes, she tugged at the bodice, smoothed the skirt, ignoring the sick churning of nerves gone awry as the reality of marrying Nick hit home, and hard.

Almost faint from anxiety, she took a deep breath, another, before opening her eyes...and gasping.

She looked like a bride.

But it wasn't the divine dress or the fancy hairdo or the immaculate make-up that made all of this real.

It was the starry-eyed expression in her frightened gaze that said it all.

In spite of every sensible thing she kept trying to tell herself, she looked like a bride on the brink of marrying the man of her dreams.

Brittany's breath caught as she stepped out of the portico and got her first glimpse of her husband-to-be.

Nick stood under a beautiful poinciana lush with vivid crimson blossoms, his black tux framed against the vibrant colour. With the sun setting behind him, casting a golden glow over everything, and the fairy lights strung around the trees in the garden just twinkling to life, the entire scene was surreal.

It shouldn't be this romantic, this enticing, this special. This wedding was all business.

Tell that to my heart, she thought as she took a tentative step, her stiletto sandals skidding as they hit the sandstone pavers.

She couldn't see Nick's expression from this distance but as she walked towards him the shadows cast from the blossoms cleared and what she saw took her breath away all over again.

Honest to goodness, undiluted happiness.

Why would he look like that?

He was the one who'd proposed this ridiculous arrangement in the first place, had made it more than clear what they'd both get out of it.

So why the ecstatic, proud expression of a man who'd just glimpsed his real bride for the first time?

Her heart hammered in time with her steps, beating a rapid

rhythm as she all but tripped towards him, eager to get this over and done with.

While the setting might be picture perfect and her groom beyond handsome, this wasn't how she'd envisioned her wedding ceremony.

Sure, the groom might be the same guy she'd imagined, but that was a lifetime ago. So much had happened, so much had changed, and she was a fool if she thought for one second that anything about this marriage resembled her dreams of years gone by.

The closer she got, the louder her heart roared until she could barely hear by the time she pulled up next to him, a nervous, trembling mess.

'You're a beautiful bride,' Nick murmured in her ear, so close his warm breath raised a trail of tiny goose bumps along her neck and she knew while this marriage might be all business on paper, she wondered how on earth she'd manage to keep it platonic in the bedroom.

'Thanks.'

She cast a nervous glance at the civilian minister in a crass white suit, and a pair of bored witnesses in hotel uniforms. Her eyes squeezed shut as she dragged air into her lungs.

How had it come to this?

A quickie wedding, empty and meaningless, to a man she'd once loved with all her heart yet who hadn't loved her enough in return, when all she'd wanted to do when she'd come home was gather enough information to secure a promotion.

'Hey, it's going to be okay.'

Nick squeezed her hand and she opened her eyes, captured by the kindness in his, kindness underlined by happiness she'd glimpsed earlier.

'Trust me.'

Trust him?

She'd trusted him with her heart.

She'd trusted him with her virginity.

And he'd sent her away anyway.

So excuse her if she was a little light in the trust stakes these days.

Taking a deep breath, she forced a smile. 'Let's get this done.'

Shadows gathered in his eyes, obliterating his joy, and she mentally kicked herself for sounding so abrupt.

He wasn't forcing her into this. She was a big girl, she'd made her own decision, and now the moment of truth had arrived she had to suck it up.

Nick gestured to the minister to start and the next fifteen minutes flew by in a blur of meaningless vows, empty promises and pretend smiles.

Her heart ached so much she almost cried, twice, but one look into Nick's determined dark eyes gave her the strength to get through it.

Until the kiss.

'You may now kiss the bride.'

The minister beamed as if he'd just bestowed the greatest gift on them, but all Brittany could think was how she'd hold it together when Nick's lips touched hers.

Her eyelids slammed shut against the threatening tears, against the determination on his face as his head descended, slowly, agonisingly slowly, when all she wanted was for this to be done with.

She wanted a quick, seal-the-deal kiss.

What she got was something else entirely as his lips brushed hers, so soft, so gentle, so tantalising, drawing her towards him like an invisible gossamer thread being gently tugged.

She couldn't break the hold, break the spell, as he bundled her in his arms and kissed her, really kissed her, with every ounce of pent-up emotion bubbling between them.

The tears started falling then, swift, coursing, raining

down her cheeks and splattering his lapels as he dabbed them away with his thumbs, his smile too warm, too tender, too understanding.

'Damn you, Mancini,' she muttered, her gaze firmly fixed on the second button of his dress shirt as she blinked rapidly.

'I feel this too, Red.'

He tilted her chin up, giving her no option but to meet his scrutinising gaze. 'Don't fight it.' She had as much chance of fighting this as receiving a welcome-home hug from her father! But she knew she mustn't give in entirely to this attraction simmering between them, couldn't give into the insane dream to make this marriage real.

She had a life in London, a promotion to nail. Then why the renewed rush of tears at the thought of leaving all this, leaving Nick, behind?

'Come on, almost done, then we can relax.'

He held her hand the entire time through the signing of the certificates, through the forced pleasantries from the minister and the false congratulations from the witnesses she didn't know, and the trip in the elevator to the fifth floor.

'Where are we going?'

Stupid question, for she knew, and every cell in her body was on high alert.

They had to have a fake wedding night for people to believe this marriage was real, she got that. The part she was having trouble with was reminding herself of the *fake* part.

'Our suite.'

Two little words that sent a tremor of longing through her as she wished she were being whisked away to a fabulous room with her husband for real.

But this wasn't real, none of it was, and she needed to keep telling herself that as he held onto her hand as if he'd never let go.

'It's one of the hotel's best. The type of room that allows

the occupants to step into a different world and lets all their fantasies come true.'

Her head snapped up at his husky tone, her skin prickling in alarm at the basest desire glittering in his eyes.

Oh, heck, why did he have to go and mention fantasies? It would've been hard enough resisting him without the added pressure of envisioning all sorts of inventive ways she could share a room with the hottest guy to walk the earth, possibly seeing him naked, his hair ruffled by sleep first thing in the morning, that sexy smile playing about his mouth…

'I'm sure the room will be fine.'

Could she sound any lamer?

'Oh, it's better than fine.'

She inhaled sharply, Nick's subtle woody aftershave that had teased her for the last hours warping her senses when she had a precarious enough hold on them as it was.

'It's the French suite. Hope you like it.'

The French suite?

Suddenly, her magnanimous decision to share a room for a faux wedding night with Nick took on a whole new meaning.

A basic, boring, run-of-the-mill room she could've handled. Something like the French suite sounded way too seductive for comfort. Though right now, with Nick palming a key card out of his pocket as they stopped outside an elaborate ivory and gold door, she had more important things to worry about.

Such as how she could keep the guy she'd loved all those years ago at arm's length.

More importantly, did she really want to?

CHAPTER SEVEN

NICK gripped Brittany's hand as he slid their room card into the slot and waited for the tiny green light to flash.

Their room.

They'd be sharing a room, tonight, their wedding night.

He could barely think of anything else as he pushed the door open and gestured to her to step inside.

'Oh, my.'

Her gasp of surprise had him standing taller. Every inch of this hotel was his idea, from the boutique-styled foyer with its casual elegance to the extensive range of 'fantasy' suites designed to please the most discerning traveller.

Having the woman he'd married, the woman whose opinion he'd always valued, admire this room filled him with pride.

'You like it?'

She nodded, her eyes wide as they swept the room, alighting on the massive four-poster king-size bed covered in gold and ivory cushions and draped in yards of filmy chiffon—he'd labelled it 'some fancy thin material' and stood corrected by the aghast interior designer who'd taken him through the hotel suite by suite when he'd first dreamed up the idea.

The memory brought a smile to his face, a smile that quickly broadened when Britt turned her wide eyes, now filled with mischief, towards him.

'Knowing your sense of humour, for a second there when you mentioned French suite I had visions of a maid's outfit hanging in the wardrobes rather than fluffy robes and baskets of…'

She trailed off, bit her tongue and he raised an eyebrow.

'Of?'

With crimson cheeks, she said, 'French letters.'

He chuckled, urged her into the room with a gentle push in the small of her back.

'I haven't heard condoms called those in years.'

She waved her hand at him. 'Forget I said anything. Speaking before I think.'

She looked adorable with her flaming cheeks and wobbly smile, in stark contrast to her wedding gown and upswept hair.

He shouldn't tease her, he really shouldn't, but he didn't have her on the back foot very often and he couldn't resist.

'If this suite is too boring, we could always change to another. The Roman room, complete with marble columns around a central spa bath right in the bedroom, is pretty nifty. Or there's the Scottish room with its lavish faux fireplace and fur rug in front of it, or if you're feeling really adventurous there's always the Tack room, complete with whips, for those who need a little added excitement in their lives.'

'Whips?'

Her voice came out a squeak and he laughed.

'Okay, so I've just invented the Tack room, but hey, what the hell, it might draw a few customers.'

'What sort of hotel are you running here?'

'I resent what you're implying, lady.'

To his surprise, the mischief had returned to her eyes as she quirked an eyebrow. 'It's wifey to you now.'

Just like that, it hit him all over again.

They were married.

It was their wedding night.

And no amount of kidding around or playing the fool would douse his driving need to consummate this marriage.

Business might be the motivator behind their nuptials but his unquenchable need to have Britt in his arms again was a definite bonus.

Taking a step closer, he ran a fingertip down her arm, delighting in the slight tremor, proving she wasn't as immune to him as she'd like him to believe.

'Wife…I like the sound of that.'

'In name only, of course.'

Her biting response might have been edgy, but she didn't move when his finger continued its leisurely exploration, reaching her shoulder, skimming along her collarbone, resting in the hollow just above where her pulse beat frantically.

'Of course,' he said, ducking his head to replace his finger with his lips, turned on by her low moan and the way her head fell back to give him better access.

Her skin tasted better than he remembered, deliciously soft with a hint of vanilla, and it took every inch of his rapidly dwindling will power not to devour her on the spot.

'This isn't supposed to happen,' she murmured as his lips trailed slowly upwards, nuzzling behind her ear, nipping the lobe before swooping on her mouth in a fiery kiss that branded her his.

Raging need exploded in him as her tongue touched his, the same overpowering, overwhelming need that had driven him to possess her years earlier.

Nothing had changed, absolutely nothing. He was still the same star-struck guy helplessly under her spell.

The realisation should've angered him, for he was nothing like the blue-collar farm boy he'd once been. But he didn't give a damn, didn't care two hoots she now had him as ready and raring for her as he'd been as a horny eighteen-year-old.

Wrenching his mouth from hers and dragging in a breath,

he captured her face in his hands, noting the swollen lips, the rosy cheeks, the eyes midnight-blue with passion, his libido roaring in response.

'You know something? This was meant to happen from the first moment you came back.'

To her credit, she didn't look away, didn't take a step back.

'You're wrong. Nothing has gone to plan since I returned.'

The flicker of pain in her eyes hit him hard and he dropped his hands, gave her space and she took it, putting enough distance between them for him to feel the loss.

'Tell me you don't want to consummate this marriage as much as I do.'

There, he threw it out, knowing the firebrand she used to be would never back down from a challenge.

However, the forlorn bride in a fancy dress staring wistfully out of the window was a far cry from the feisty girl he'd known, and the thought he'd made her this unhappy was a kick in the guts. And the wake-up call he needed.

'Forget it. I'm going out for a while. I'll be back later.'

Failure didn't sit well with him, never had, and, hating how he'd botched this, he wrenched open the door.

'Nick, wait!'

But he didn't.

He walked out on his bride and slammed the door shut on his dreams of a memorable wedding night.

Brittany kicked off her sandals, ripped off the wedding dress and tore the frangipani from her hair, crushing it in her palm in the process.

She stared at the furrowed flower, limp, lifeless, and sank onto the bed, letting the petals drift from her fingertips to the floor.

She was like that flower: all pristine and showy on the outside, a crumpled mess on the inside.

As if getting through the ceremony hadn't been hard enough, pretending she didn't want a real wedding night had almost driven her insane.

Nick wanted her.

She wanted Nick.

Where was the problem?

A sharp pain shot through her chest as a timely reminder of exactly what the problem was: her heart. Her stupid, impressionable, just-break-me-now heart that jumped up and said 'pick me, pick me' every time Nick Mancini looked her way.

It'd been the same ten years ago and nothing had changed. She'd been home just over a week, long enough to realise singing the 'I'm only doing this for business' tune wouldn't cut it with Nick.

Not this time.

He'd let her walk away back then, he'd let her do it now, so why was she falling for him regardless?

With a frustrated groan, she headed for the bathroom. A good, long soak might ease her tension.

Yeah, right, just as trying to date other guys had eradicated Nick from her memory banks. Not a chance in hell.

While the bath filled she paced the bathroom, fiddling with the fancy toiletries, picking them up, putting them down, trying not to stare at her reflection as she did so.

The odd times she caught a glimpse in the disastrously monstrous mirrors, she didn't like what she saw.

A woman in sexy lingerie with thoroughly kissed lips, shining eyes and a glow no amount of blush could induce.

A woman who'd subconsciously bought the sheer ivory lace demi-cup bra and matching knickers edged in rosebuds in the hope the man she still fancied might get to see it.

A woman who was kidding herself.

That stung most of all, the fact she was a smart, astute businesswoman yet here she was playing silly games with herself.

She wanted Nick.

It all came back to that.

Her job and the promotion might be the reason she was here but right now, this very second, Nick was her motivation for staying in this suite when she could've quite as easily escaped.

She hated manipulation, hated lies: dear old Dad had seen to that. So why was she wasting time lying to herself now? She'd be gone in a few months, back to her orderly life. Why not make the most of the time they had?

For if she slept with Nick or not, spending the next eight weeks with him would break her heart regardless. At least this way she'd have some fun.

After closing off the gold taps, she carefully slipped out of the lingerie—she had high hopes for the stuff now—and dipped under the lavender-scented bubbles to her neck, resting her head against the giant Jacuzzi and sighing with pleasure.

Closing her eyes, she savoured the lavender scent infusing her senses, soothing, relaxing, helping her mind wander. And wander it did, taking a stroll down memory lane, to the first time Nick had made love to her.

Inviting her to dinner at the plantation when Papa had taken a business trip to Brisbane, the lukewarm pizza they'd fed each other while sitting on the frayed love seat on the back veranda, the icy cola fizzing up out of the can and dousing her in stickiness, Nick's tongue licking it off her...

He'd made her first time beyond special. He'd been caring and gentle and amazing, treating her virginity like a precious gift she'd given him.

She'd never forgotten it, never forgotten him and it was high time she stopped pretending she didn't want to recreate the magic they'd once shared between the sheets.

Sinking under water to sluice away her memories, she thought she'd done a fair job by the time she resurfaced.

Until she opened her eyes and saw Nick leaning against the bathroom door, staring at her with barely disguised lust in his incredible dark eyes, looking like a man in definite need of a bath.

CHAPTER EIGHT

NICK took several surreptitious breaths, willing his pulse to slow and his heart to stop pounding. At this rate, he'd collapse on the spot if it kept thumping with such ferocity.

'You came back.'

Her tentative smile had him gripping the door jamb to stop from striding across the bathroom, sweeping her out of the bath and holding her close.

Thankfully, only her head was visible, the rest of her delectable body submerged under a bubble cover that threatened to spill out onto the black-and-white-tiled floor. Not that the bubbles hampered his imagination. He could picture exactly what delights were hidden beneath those bubbles and the images weren't helping his heart rate.

'Yeah, couldn't stay away.'

'I'm glad.'

Her tongue flicked out to moisten her bottom lip in a totally innocuous gesture that slammed into his conscious like a bull ramming a gate in mating season.

'Are you?'

He was too old to play guessing games, too wound up to figure out why the turnaround.

He'd come back because this was his wedding night and, while lust might have temporarily blinded him to the real reason behind this marriage, the sight of more international guests checking into the hotel had alerted him to the fact he needed to make this marriage look real for investors to accept him as one of their own.

It was the reason he'd come up with this crazy scheme in the first place but somewhere along the line—probably around the time he'd first set eyes on his beautiful bride—his motivation had blurred until all he could see was Britt.

She nodded, gathering more bubbles with her hands on the surface and bringing them towards her chest. Damn, what he'd give for a fan now.

'Uh-huh. I didn't like how things ended before. Why don't you let me finish up in here and we can talk?'

Talk? She wanted to *talk*?

With that small smile curving her lips, droplets clinging to her eyelashes and her hair falling in tendrils around her face—he wasn't even going near those damn bubbles—talk was the furthest thing from his mind.

The corners of her mouth twitched as if she knew exactly what he was thinking and he quickly thrust his hands in his pockets and back-pedalled a few steps.

'Fine.'

'Give me five minutes and I'll be out.'

Her smile could've fogged up the mirror a lot more than the fragrant steam rising from the water and he managed a terse nod before backing out and closing the door.

Damn it, why hadn't she closed the door in the first place? Didn't she know the effect she had on him?

Of course she did. Then why the nasty thought that suddenly insinuated its way into his lust-hazed brain, making him see sense in her behaviour.

Since she'd arrived, she hadn't shown much interest in him as a man. Sure, she'd teased him, but that was nothing new, she'd always done that. The teasing often included flirting but that came naturally too.

He'd been the one to kiss her when she'd first arrived home.

He'd wanted to kiss her after dinner at his place and she'd pulled away.

He'd wanted to share a room tonight; by her reaction earlier it was pretty obvious she didn't.

Sure, she'd responded to his kisses, but maybe that had been for old times' sake? Giving in to him not to antagonise him, not to jeopardise their deal and her precious promotion? Made sense.

In reality, how far did he want to take this?

She'd be gone once her business here was finished, back to her high life in London, and he'd be left behind again, pretending he had a modern marriage where two busy business people lived on opposite sides of the planet.

He'd let her walk away last time, didn't tell her the truth; what would be different now?

Shaking his head, he took off his tux, pulled a T-shirt over his head, stepped into jeans, ran a comb through his hair and added a splash of aftershave. He would've loved a shower but the thought of using the bathroom so soon after Britt had vacated it, her scent lingering everywhere, evidence of her presence all over, would be too much.

She wanted to talk.

That was a sure-fire libido-killer. In his experience, when women wanted to 'talk' they wanted to lay down the law.

Well, whatever she had to say, he'd deal with it. Just as he'd deal with this crazy, one-sided obsession to make their marriage real.

After brushing her teeth, Brittany took a final look in the mirror: without make-up, the freckles on her nose stood out like sprinkles on a cupcake, her loose hair had turned frizzy courtesy of the humidity and her plain cotton PJs wouldn't win any Victoria's Secret competitions.

Just the look she'd aimed for…before she'd taken a bath and had that little revelation to make the most of the next two months with the sexiest guy to walk the planet.

Her bad boy.

Who was doing his best to appear good but she knew better, knew the underlying rebellious streak that lent him a dangerous edge she found infinitely appealing.

Most girls went through a bad-boy phase, lusting after guys they shouldn't and couldn't have, guys with attitude, guys you wouldn't dare bring home to meet the folks.

Nick had been her James Dean, Marlon Brando and Sean Penn all rolled into one and, while the designer suits and air of success had softened the edges, she just knew he was the same sexy rebel underneath.

But it was more than that, so much more, and the fact her heart had squeezed every time he'd entered a room these last few days was proof enough she'd developed a monstrous crush on her rebel with a cause all over again.

A crush she finally planned to fully indulge. However, there was one main problem. The pyjamas she'd brought were a deeply unsexy pair she'd bought especially to appear as unappealing as possible. Her body, humming with the heat of the bath and anticipation, informed her point-blank that fuchsia stripes wouldn't do the job.

As for the lingerie she'd intended on using to prove her point tonight, it had taken a tumble into the sink while she'd been brushing her teeth and there was no way she was walking into their bedroom wearing wet, see-through, ivory lace. That left only one viable option.

Wrapping the oversized bathrobe around her damp, overexcited body, she took a deep breath and prepared to leave the safe haven of the gloriously tiled bathroom.

Only a robe between her and Nick. As if she weren't nervous enough.

Nick had his back to her and she was darn grateful for that extra shot of oxygen a second ago, for the moment she caught sight of him her lungs seized.

Soft black cotton moulded to his broad shoulders, hugging the muscular contours of his back before tapering to a narrow waist, tucked into faded denim...

That was all he used to wear ten years ago, black T-shirts and denim, somewhat of a clichéd bad-boy outfit, but she'd never cared. He'd always looked delectable and nothing had changed.

With her eyes fixed on his butt, she must've made some terribly embarrassing sound akin to a groan for he turned, his gaze zeroing in on her damp, bare skin, what little there was on show. His eyes turned very dark brown and he swallowed.

Brittany smiled wickedly at him, his reaction fuelling her faltering courage.

He shook his head as if to break himself out of a trance, cleared his throat, and finally spoke in a low, dangerous tone.

'Just so you know—if you're planning on avoiding being seduced, you'll definitely need more than a robe. Maybe an entire wardrobe.' His voice sounded strained.

Brittany could see the bad boy inside was only barely contained. Just the thought of what might happen when he broke out added further to her inner tremblings. In a voice that sounded higher than her own, she said, 'Well, I wanted to talk about that—'

'Yes?'

His response was so fast it interrupted her mid-sentence, and she gaped at him like an idiot for a moment, her train of thought derailed.

'You were saying? Something about seducing me?'

His wide grin broke the tension as she remembered how much she liked this man and she grinned back.

'You wish.'

'You have no idea how much.'

His intense tone caused her belly to drop in a frightening free fall as liquid heat pooled in places long ignored, every inch of her hungry body on high alert as the bed dipped when he sat next to her.

While her scrambled brains tried to reform the words she was having such a hard time articulating, he sighed.

'But I thought about it, and you were right.'

What? No! She opened her mouth but he continued before she could speak.

'Let me guess. You're not interested in changing the status quo between us. You don't want to ruin a good working relationship. You don't want to risk wrecking our deal by letting sex get in the way of the sound business decision we've made, right?'

Wrong. Wrong, wrong, wrong!

Logically, he made perfect sense and he'd reiterated the arguments she'd been having with herself ever since she'd said yes to his ridiculous proposal.

Emotionally, she wanted to rant and scream and kick her Garfield slippers into the Great Barrier Reef, for now she'd made up her mind to alleviate some of this growing tension between them she didn't want to take the safe, sensible option any more.

But what could she say?

Backing down from her previous stance would make her seem fickle and indecisive and decidedly stupid, not to mention shooting down any credibility in convincing him her acceptance of his proposal was one hundred per cent business.

For him, having sex would be satisfying his lust factor. For her, it was so much more and he'd know it. She'd told him so ten years earlier and knowing Nick he wouldn't have forgotten.

'Just business, right?'

With a sinking heart, she nodded.

'Right.'

'Okay, then, glad we got that settled.'

He didn't move and when she raised her eyes to his she knew nothing was settled, far from it, for while Nick might be spouting the business tune his eyes were gobbling her up and coming back for seconds.

'Britt?'

She gulped, knowing her voice would come out squeaky if she didn't, for the longer he looked at her like that, the harder it was to breathe.

'Yeah?'

'You made a breathtaking bride.'

It wasn't his compliment that made her blush as much as the memory of how she'd envisioned him taking her wedding dress off.

'The dress was pretty special—'

'I wasn't talking about the dress.'

His hand snaked across the bed and rested on hers, the simple touch setting her body alight as her gaze flew to his, connected, locked, unable to look away even if she wanted to.

Tension crackled between them as she wavered between yanking her hand out from under his to re-establish equilibrium and closing the short distance between them and straddling his lap.

'You're still the most beautiful woman I've ever seen.'

A soft, wistful sigh escaped her lips, a sigh filled with hope and fear and wishes that things could be different for them, that this could be a real wedding night in every sense of the word.

Mustering a smile, she said, 'And you're still the charmer.'

He winked. 'Is it working?'

'Depends why you're trying to charm me.'

'Ah…the million-dollar question…'

Rather than releasing her hand, his thumb traced slow circles on the back of it, grazing her knuckles, dipping into the grooves, sending heat spiralling through her body.

Her eyes drifted shut, as if she could block out his touch and what it was doing to her body, but if anything the sensations increased tenfold.

Every nerve ending snapped to attention with every minute caress, every muscle liquefied with the barest brush of his thumb, and when he stroked her fingers from knuckle to tip the tension strumming her body coalesced into a fiery yearning that had her leaping off the bed like he'd prodded her.

'I'm really tired.'

His knowing gaze told her he knew exactly why she'd retreated, yet thankfully he didn't push it.

'Okay then. Do you want to have supper? I can get Room Service to bring us up something, or would you prefer bed?'

To her endless embarrassment, she blushed and scooted around to the other side of the bed, the very mention of which made her feel like a schoolgirl jilted by the high-school jock.

'I'm not hungry.'

She slid under the six-hundred-thread-count sheets. The sooner she feigned sleep, the sooner she could avoid looking at his delicious body and wishing he were supper.

'You sure?'

His deep, husky tone had her imagining warmed honey drizzled across his torso and strawberries dipped in chocolate nestled in his navel and she swallowed, at serious risk of drooling.

'I'm sure. Now, if you don't mind, I need some rest. So scoot.'

'Huh?'

'The couch? You know, that thing next to the table over there?'

He shook his head and sent her his best puppy-dog look, the one he'd perfected back in high school, the same one that melted her heart.

'I can't sleep on that. It doesn't convert into a sofa bed, it's two feet too short and has rocks under the cushions.'

'Well, you can't expect me to sleep there!'

And she'd be a fool to consider letting him share the bed. By the longing look he cast at the bed, she wouldn't have much choice.

'Red, as attractive as you look in the contraception-on-legs robe, this bed is big enough to fit four people. I'm sure we can share without getting into too much trouble.'

She almost would have believed him, if the last few tension-filled minutes hadn't happened. They might've agreed to a sex-free wedding night but, with her belly tumbling with nerves, her skin prickling with heat and the rest of her buzzing from repressed need, she knew trouble was only a tumble in the sack away.

But what choice did she have? She couldn't subject him to a sleepless night, it just wouldn't be fair. Or mature.

She could do this. Sharing a bed with Nick would be like having a friend over for a slumber party. And guaranteed she'd be the one spending a sleepless night!

'We can put pillows down the middle if you think that'll help.'

He grinned, a fully-fledged teasing grin that mocked her, and she briefly wondered what had happened to her bath pep talk. Lying in the giant bed with the sheets almost pulled up to her neck like a blushing virgin screamed prude and not the sassy city girl she liked to think herself.

Why couldn't she share a bed with Nick and consider it in a non-sexual way?

Because she wanted him! Bad.

That was when it hit her.

If she couldn't tell him what she wanted, what if she showed him by giving him a little bit of that teasing he was so good at?

She sat up straighter, allowing the sheet to dip, revealing the robe's gaping neckline, and sent him a smile that could've tempted a eunuch.

'No pillows needed. I'll keep my hands to myself, promise.'

To her surprise, his cocky grin slipped, as if he hadn't expected her to agree with him, let alone flirt right back.

Oh, yeah, this could be fun!

'You better not grope me in my sleep,' he muttered, sending her an almost hopeful look she'd do exactly that.

'Hands off, remember?'

'In that case, move over.'

Okay, so they'd settled the sleeping arrangements fairly painlessly. Good. This wouldn't be too difficult.

Think slumber party. Think friends. Think harmless fun. Easy.

However, the instant she dropped her guard, Nick did something to shock her all over again.

'What are you doing?' she shrieked as he undid the zip on his jeans and shucked out of them, standing next to the bed wearing the sexiest, briefest pair of black silk boxers she'd ever seen.

'I'm getting ready for bed. You don't expect me to sleep in jeans, do you?'

'N-no, but don't you own PJs?'

He shook his head, looking proud of the fact as she struggled to keep her gaze averted from those boxers and the lean, muscled legs beneath them. Sheesh, he looked good enough to eat—and she definitely wouldn't go there!

'Too hot. Besides, you should be grateful. I usually sleep nude.'

That shut her up as she closed her eyes and prayed for a miracle.

Her slumber-party theory wasn't working, not with Nick standing there in his underwear. His very sexy underwear.

'Trying to imagine what I'd look like, huh? Well, if you open your eyes, I can give you a demo—'

'No!' she yelled, her eyes flying open against her will in the faint hope he'd go through with his threat. 'Just get under the damn sheets and keep your underwear on.'

'Your loss.'

He had the audacity to shrug out of his T, toss it on a chair and slide in next to her, sending a dazzling smile in the process. Cocky, brash and totally shameless.

The next ten hours were going to be hell. Or heaven, depending how she looked at it, and right now, with an amazing expanse of broad, tanned chest on display, heaven seemed uncomfortably closer to the mark. "Night, Red. Pleasant dreams.'

As if.

Pleasant would be the last word she'd use to describe what she knew would be an erotic kaleidoscope of images that would plague her all night long.

She turned off the lamp, grateful she couldn't see him any more. Not that she needed to. The image of Nick standing next to the bed wearing nothing but those black boxers and a smile would be a memory to treasure for years to come.

'Can I ask you something?'

She sighed and rolled over to face him, her eyes adjusting to the darkness slowly and just able to make out his reclining form at a safe distance across the bed.

Though were a few feet really safe? This was Nick Mancini she was sharing a bed with, *the* Nick Mancini she'd loved as a teenager and missed for years.

'You will anyway, so go ahead.'

'Why did you run away?'

'I didn't.'

The defensive words popped out before she thought about it, an instant response to a subject she'd rather avoid.

'Yeah, you did.'

His whisper floated on the darkness, a mixture of accusation and regret, and she wondered how he'd felt at the time.

When she'd first arrived in London, she'd been too busy coping with her own hurt to think about anything else. The people she loved in her life kept hurting her: her dad, then

Nick, and she'd struggled to hold together while trying to build a new life.

Part of her coping strategy had been to paint Nick in a bad light: he wasn't worthy of her; he didn't care; he wasn't capable of emotions.

But what if she'd been wrong?

What if he had cared and there was another reason behind his refusal to accompany her? After all, she'd hidden her real reason for fleeing.

'I just needed a new start.'

Which was partially true. She just couldn't tell him the reason behind her desperate yearning for a new start.

'But why London? You hung around Brisbane for a month before you left—you could've stayed there. Even Sydney or Melbourne at a pinch, places where we could've kept in contact, tried to maintain a re…' He trailed off and she resisted the urge to sit bolt upright and flick the light on.

Had she heard right? Was he saying they could've had a relationship if she hadn't wanted to get as far away from her father as possible?

'Maintain a what?' she prompted, eager to hear the words but almost wishing he wouldn't say them.

What was the point of bringing all this up now? She couldn't change the past, couldn't change what she'd done, and knowing she could've had a future with Nick even outside Jacaranda would hurt her all over again.

'A really strong friendship,' he finished, and disappointment pierced her.

So what? Wasn't that better than hearing he might've loved her back then as much as she'd loved him?

'I know I acted like a jerk before you left, I know we had our share of troubles, but we were really good friends. I missed that after you left.'

Wow, he'd missed her. And actually admitted it!

Time to lighten the mood before she lost her head completely, blurted out the truth and sought comfort in his strong arms.

'Aw, shucks. I didn't think you cared.'

'I cared.'

His two little words hung in the growing silence between them, laden with untold truths and forgotten dreams. 'But, hey, life happens.'

This time, he broke the tension with a forced chuckle. 'We've both come a long way. And however many times I tied your hair to a chair or put frogs in your bag, I still care. Goodnight.'

Nick's admission filled her with a slow, delicious warmth that seeped through her body, leaving her cocooned in a delightful haze.

How could she maintain her immunity when he said stuff like that? Better yet, did she want to?

'Don't let the bed bugs bite,' she murmured, snuggling under the sheets and closing her eyes, hoping for sleep and knowing it was useless.

She had too much to think about, starting with her reawakening feelings for a man best left in her past.

CHAPTER NINE

NICK stirred some time around midnight, his dreamless sleep disturbed by a puff of air somewhere in the vicinity of his ear lobe.

His eyelids cranked open a fraction, half-heartedly investigating the source of air, only to snap open as he registered a luscious woman draped over his upper torso, her arm flung proprietorially across his chest and a leg nudging the vicinity of his boxers.

Not just any woman.

Britt.

His wife.

Whom he wanted to make love to something fierce.

Considering the chaste way they'd fallen asleep he should gently slip out from under her and try not to wake her.

But his good intentions evaporated when she snuggled closer, her knee edging towards a fast-growing hard-on, and he froze, gritting his teeth to stop from groaning out loud.

He could play the gentleman, but where would be the fun in that? Britt had always called him her bad boy and, while a small part of him had thought she only hung around him because she was tempted to slum it for a while, he'd liked the reputation.

And it had grown, fuelled by idle gossip of small-town inhabitants and the fact he smoked, rode a motorbike and lived in denim.

He'd heard the rumours, from his fictitious tattoo of skull-and-crossbones on his butt to riding bare-chested all the way to Sydney.

He'd laughed, silently appalled at how reputations could be made or broken by hearsay. Considering he'd been working his ass off trying to make the plantation stay afloat at the time, he hadn't much cared.

Another puff of air, another small moan in her sleep had him easing away before he did something she'd regret. Make no mistake, she'd been about to give him the 'don't think you can seduce me' talk last night before he'd cut her off. As if he wouldn't have got the message from seeing her in that libido-killing bulky robe.

She'd made her point earlier and he'd be damned if he sat through it again, rehashing stuff he didn't agree with. Especially when she was half naked, with all the distraction that would have entailed. The way he saw it, they could keep this marriage business focused while having fun too but there was no way, no how, he'd be pushing the issue now.

Britt had made her feelings more than clear.

'Nick?'

Her sleepy whisper slammed into his consciousness, beckoning him to stay right where he was. But he couldn't, he wouldn't take advantage of the situation no matter how turned on he was or how badly he wanted his wife.

'Shh, go back to sleep.'

He stroked her hair, a small part of him melting as she snuggled deeper and, rather than pull away, he cuddled her closer with his arm.

Her hair tickled his shoulder, her cheek, so soft and warm, pressed against his chest and the faintest scent of lavender and vanilla lulled him into believing that, for now, this was enough.

* * *

If Nick was a bad boy, Brittany was a bad girl.

A very bad girl.

When she'd woken in Nick's arms that first morning, she'd felt him pulling away, sensed him trying to disengage. And while winding up with her head resting on his chest and the rest of her draped over him hadn't been planned, she'd taken full advantage of the situation.

Maybe not *full* advantage, as that would've entailed doing a lot more than cuddling, but she'd pretended to sleep while savouring the hard chest cushioning her cheek, the warm, toned body beneath her hands and his intensely male scent, which set off her pheromones in a big way and always had.

She could've stopped there but, no, she'd been a really, really bad girl.

And proceeded to do the same thing every morning.

For the next two weeks.

The tension was killing her. If only it were doing the same to her husband.

'How's business coming along?'

Her head snapped up from where she'd been resting her chin in her hands, staring out of the window and daydreaming of exactly how bad she'd like to be, to find the object of her wicked fantasies staring at her with cool detachment.

It had to be a ruse. After all, wasn't he the one who'd been hot to trot on their wedding night? Surely he couldn't have turned off just like that?

By his compressed lips and grim expression, apparently so.

Feigning nonchalance she didn't feel, she waved her hand towards the stack of paperwork on the table in front of her.

'The photographer's been out to the plantation every day this week and taken loads of shots. The cameraman's due out there tomorrow, and I'm collating some of the historical info

I got from your grandfather's ledgers. So everything's coming along nicely.'

He crossed the room, perched on the edge of the table, her eyes now level with his crotch, and she quickly stood, not needing to look *there* considering she'd been having bad thoughts a few moments ago.

'You've been busy.'

'Loads to do. I've got a task list a mile long today, including heading out to the plantation to scout more locations, checking the ones I've already chosen, making sure they match the information I'm in the process of adding to the pitch—'

'Hang on.'

His hand shot out, gripping hers and preventing her from putting some much-needed distance between them.

Trying not to show how much his simple touch affected her, she raised an eyebrow.

'What's up?'

Shaking his head, he squeezed her hand before releasing it. 'I'm no good at this.'

'At what?'

'This whole fake marriage thing.'

'Oh, thaaat.'

Well, well, well, maybe the tension was getting to him after all.

'Not used to sharing a suite, huh?'

He must've heard her teasing tone but rather than smile, he fixed her with a piercing stare.

'Not used to sharing a suite with you.'

Right then she knew, no matter how cool Nick was playing it, how busy he was, he was just as rattled by their underlying attraction as she was.

'Oh? I thought it'd be a breeze.'

She waltzed around the room, picking up floral skirts and summer dresses and the odd piece of lingerie or two.

Okay, so she wasn't playing fair with the lingerie but, hey, she wanted to get a reaction out of him, and if the tortured look that flickered across his face as she twirled an ebony satin bra on the end of her finger before tossing it into a drawer was any indication, her plan was working.

'A breeze? More like a damn tropical cyclone,' he muttered, shoving off the table and heading for the wide window affording a glorious view of Noosa beach.

'I'm getting to you, aren't I?'

She snuck up behind him, just stopping short of sliding her arms around his waist and laying her head against his back.

He didn't turn, keeping his gaze fixed on the stunning view.

'I guess this business arrangement of ours isn't quite what I expected.'

'That's because we share a past, you dufus.'

Oops. Had she really said that out loud?

By the speed at which he turned to face her, she had.

An endearing smile curled his lips. 'Dufus?'

'I've called you worse.'

His eyes darkened as they hovered on her mouth, as if he was remembering everything she'd ever called him and more.

'Yeah, I remember.'

She'd come this far, might as well go for broke.

'What else do you remember?'

Silence stretched between them, surprising her. Nick might be many things, but chicken wasn't one of them. She'd called his bluff, expecting some kind of answer even if it was a dismissive smart-ass remark.

Just when she'd given up, he finally reached out and twirled a strand of her hair around his finger.

'I remember you wore your hair long, to your waist. I

remember how you used to squeal on the back of my bike as I rounded the bends.'

He tugged on her hair, bringing her closer…and closer… and closer until there was a whisper between them.

'But most of all, I remember how you made me feel back then.'

Unexpected emotion clogged her throat, effectively clouding her sweep-me-into-your-arms fantasy.

She'd wanted to prove the sizzle existed between them, wanted to tease him, wanted to get a reaction out of him. The last thing she'd expected was this serious trip down memory lane from a guy who acted as if they didn't have a past most of the time.

'How did I make you feel?'

He was so close his breath feathered her lips, sending a ripple of longing so intense through her it took her breath away.

'Like I could make all our dreams come true.'

She sighed, wishing he hadn't pushed her away, wishing he'd said yes when she'd asked him to move away with her all those years ago, wishing he had made her dreams come true.

He was all she'd ever wanted, until her freedom became all important.

She'd thought she'd had it all, convinced he'd move to London and they'd have the life they wanted. Until he'd withdrawn from her, shutting her out emotionally, physically, citing work and study and family as a means not to see her.

She'd persisted, convinced they were meant to be together, captivated by the occasional glimpse of the guy she'd fallen in love with, wary of what he'd become the harder she pushed for them to leave town.

Her dreams had been big, had been big enough for both of them. But Nick wasn't the dream-maker she'd been foolish once to believe he was.

Acknowledging their attraction was one thing, opening

her heart another, and while she wanted him now more than ever she knew nothing had changed.

He still wouldn't follow her to London even if she were crazy enough to ask.

'Nick, I don't think—'

'Then don't. Think, that is,' he murmured, a second before his lips locked on hers in the softest heartbreaking kiss that reached all the way down to her soul.

It lasted less than a few seconds, a fleeting glimpse of tenderness rarely seen from this passionate man, and when he raised his head, brushed her bottom lip with a fingertip and walked away, she was left reeling.

Reeling with the knowledge she still believed in dreams.

And his ability to make all hers come true.

Nick entered the marquee, his gaze immediately drawn to the stunning woman in a white dress chatting to the richest guy in the State.

Brittany looked incredible, a soft, clingy Grecian-style dress fastened on one shoulder with a silver clip, leaving her other deliciously bare, her hair piled up with soft golden streaks falling softly around her face and just enough make-up to enhance her beauty.

Hell. Just looking at her from a distance was making him crazy; what hope did he have up close?

Sure, she looked like a supermodel tonight but he still couldn't erase the image of her clad in that supersized robe on their wedding night.

He'd lied about the robe being contraception on legs. The minute he'd caught his first glimpse of her, framed in the bathroom doorway with vulnerability written all over her face, he'd wanted to cross the room, haul her into his arms and never let go.

That had been one hell of a night.

Not for the reason he might've anticipated, considering she fired his libido as no other woman ever had or probably ever would.

He'd lain awake for hours, listening to the soft sounds of her breathing, wishing things could've turned out differently between them, silently chastising himself for being a bloody fool.

He'd thought by getting her to talk about the past, she might relax, learn to trust him again. Instead, she'd fed him some lame excuse about why she'd run away and he'd been the stupid one to blurt out he still cared. Go figure?

Thankfully, the last fortnight had passed in a frenetic blur with finalising details for the new Caribbean hotel and, apart from that slight aberration yesterday when he'd almost made a pathetic declaration of how much he liked having her around, they'd managed to maintain a polite distance.

All business, which was exactly why she'd agreed to accompany him to the Bachelor and Spinsters Ball tonight. A ball the Phant-A-Sea chain was sponsoring, a ball where every billionaire in Australasia would be in attendance, a ball where he'd learn how far his plan to marry Britt had got him.

Hotel occupancy was up fifty per cent, phone calls from potential investors tripling since he'd married. Maybe the old-school tycoons had finally recognised him as a successful, wealthy businessman with one thing on his mind: making his hotels the best in the world.

Tonight would prove how far he'd come, for calling him was one thing, accepting him as one of their own in public another.

Britt glanced up at that moment and their gazes locked, hot, intense, and he strode across the harvesting shed, which looked like a cross between a country-and-western saloon and a high-school disco.

It would be the plantation's final hurrah, for once Britt had

completed her work here he'd sell the place, sever ties to his
past once and for all.

He'd prevaricated for the last twelve months, plagued by
guilt. This place had been Papa's pride and joy, built from the
ground up with grit, sweat and determination. It had been the
only place he'd ever called home but, more than that, it had
been a refuge after his mum had abandoned them.

The old farmhouse should've repulsed him, should've been
a constant reminder of what happened when he loved a
woman too much.

But he'd deliberately blocked out the few memories of his
mum, had filled his head and his heart with new ones, mostly
centred on a wizened Italian man with a penchant for ripe
tomatoes, coarse wine and sugar in his veins.

Papa had been more than a parent, he'd been his idol. The
thought of bringing shame to the family name had stopped
him from taking his rebel image too far, Papa's steadfast
support a constant reminder that he could be anybody he
chose to be.

But that was the problem.

As long as he held onto the plantation, people would be
reminded of his humble beginnings, would still harbour
doubts about his ability to mix it with the big boys.

It would kill him to sell, would tear him clean in two, but
nothing could take away memories of a father who'd helped
mould him into the man he was today.

Papa would've understood, would've encouraged him to
move forward, and that was exactly what he would do, despite
the nagging gut feeling he was turning his back on family.

'Well, if it isn't the man of the moment. Glad you finally
showed up at your own shindig, Mancini.'

To his amazement, Bram Rutger stuck his hand out,
something he'd never done despite the many times they'd

crossed paths at similar functions in Sydney or Singapore the last few years.

He shook it, vindicated his plan had worked yet despising himself for caring what this pompous old fool thought of him.

'Business, you know how it is.'

'That I do, my boy. Something we'll discuss more of when you return my phone calls. I'm looking to expand my investment portfolio and I think we should talk.'

Bram's announcement reinforced he'd made a sound business decision in marrying Britt, but his satisfaction evaporated when the old fool slipped an arm around Britt's waist.

'And I hear congratulations are in order. You've picked a fine woman here.'

Bram squeezed Britt's waist as Nick's hands squeezed into fists. 'I've known young Brittany since she was in the cradle, so make sure you take good care of her, you hear?'

Oh, he'd take good care of her, starting with punching the supercilious coot in the nose, but he forced a smile and nodded.

'Shall do. Now, if you'll excuse us?'

He held out a hand, biting back a grin when Britt all but bolted out of Bram's hold. 'Nice seeing you again, Bram.'

She wiggled her fingers in a teasing wave and Nick growled under his breath as they walked away.

'You shouldn't tease the old goat. Might give him a heart attack.'

Her cheeky smile lit up her face. 'Well, then, his kids will thank me. Apparently he's worth billions these days.'

'You're incorrigible.'

She quirked an eyebrow. 'This, coming from the guy who used to do very poor impersonations of Bram and his cronies?'

She shook her head. 'You've changed. Become a snob like them.'

'This, coming from the girl who wouldn't sit down by Jacaranda River unless I'd spread out a blanket first? From the girl who wouldn't hop on the back of my bike unless I made sure there wasn't a dot of grease on the seat? From the girl who—'

'Okay, okay, I get your point. Sheesh.'

She reached out, smoothed a lapel, her innocuous touch enough to fire his blood and set his heart pounding.

'Nice tux, by the way. Very debonair.'

'Glad you noticed.'

Their gazes locked again and this time he didn't look away.

He'd already got what he came for tonight: vindication he'd made it into the big league, recognition he was more than the blue-collar farm boy he'd once been.

Time to get this party really started.

'Come with me.'

'Where?'

'Does it matter?'

She shook her head, the tendrils framing her face swaying gently and beckoning him to reach out and twist one around his finger, draw her close and hold her all night. But there was plenty of time for that. For now, he'd settle for getting her alone and kissing her senseless.

'Come on.'

He grabbed her hand and they fought their way through the crowd. He was surprised by the turnout, hundreds of well-dressed revellers who had descended on his property, bringing their own supplies, including tents for camping overnight.

Singles balls were all the rage these days and, while he liked seeing people having fun, a huge part of him was relieved he was no longer a bachelor.

It wasn't everything it was cracked up to be, especially now he had a fortune behind him, with the women who'd once shunned him for having grease on his hands and dust in his hair clambering for a date—or, worse, a relationship.

Britt had never been like that; she'd liked him regardless

and the thought sent a burst of warmth through him, urging him to pick up the pace.

'Great turnout, huh?'

With her blue eyes glittering with excitement, she looked like a society hostess basking in the success of an event. 'And the film crew are getting loads of footage I can use in my pitch.'

'That's great, though personally I can't believe there are so many desperadoes out there.'

'Most people are here to party, not pick up.'

They caught sight of a couple kissing in the back of a ute at the same time and Britt chuckled. 'Well, most of them.'

'Get a room,' he muttered, suddenly annoyed by the sight of the amorous couple doing exactly what he'd like to be doing with the gorgeous woman by his side.

'What for? If they're anything like us, a room won't sweeten the mood.'

He risked a quick glance at her face, wondering if she were serious but, by the cheeky smile tugging at the corners of her glossed mouth, she wasn't.

'The room doesn't matter to us because we have an arrangement. And we're friends.'

More the pity. Though he planned to change all that, starting tonight.

'So are those two, by the look of it. *Good* friends.' She chuckled and slipped her hand around his elbow, a casual gesture that shouldn't have sent the blood rushing to his groin. But it did and he could barely focus on anything other than the way she smelt and how she felt tucked in to his side.

Having her stand so close to him, her signature vanilla enveloping him in seductive sweetness, was hard enough to tolerate without her smoky midnight eyes sending him signals he knew were all in his own head.

'So what did you want to show me?'

'It's in here.'

He all but dragged her through the back door into the dimly lit kitchen, knowing this was crazy but unable to stop.

Her soft laughter echoed in the empty room, his favourite in the house. He had a lifetime of family memories here: making ravioli from scratch while his dad pored over the Sunday newspapers, Britt poking her tongue out at him from across the table as she lobbed a bread roll and feigned innocence.

Yeah, this room was a definite favourite and he was about to add another treasured memory.

'Okay, apart from this place needing some light, what's the prob—?'

Nick covered her mouth with his, cutting off her words and sliding his arms around her waist, marvelling at how right this felt.

Rather than protest and try to shove him off, she groaned and wrapped her arms around his neck, opening her lips beneath his, teasing him to pleasure her, to taste her and come back for more.

He was more than willing to comply, deepening the kiss to the point where he couldn't breathe, couldn't think, couldn't feel anything beyond this incredible woman in this unforgettable moment.

She hung on tight, her hands stroking his neck, tugging him closer until he could feel the heat of her skin through his dress shirt, the sizzling, wicked heat urging him to back her up against the table and do what he'd wanted to do for weeks now.

Make sweet love to his beautiful bride.

He must've moved a fraction for she groaned, brushing her breasts against his chest, and he slid his hands around her ribcage, filling them with her full breasts, caressing them, skimming the peaks with his palms until she murmured incoherently, almost making him explode on the spot.

Alarm bells clamoured in his head—what happened to just business? What happened to getting her to make the first move this time? And he happily ignored them, allowing himself this one brief taste of pleasure before sanity returned and he'd be forced to apologise for making a complete jackass of himself.

She sensed his hesitation, for she broke the kiss, only to snuggle into his neck and playfully nip the sensitive skin there.

'I can see your problem.'

'What's that?'

His hands glided over the slinky material of her dress to caress her butt, the heat of her scorching his palms through the thin silk of her dress.

'You've got the hots for me.'

She chuckled, the small sexy laugh of a confident woman who knew exactly what sort of a schmuck she was dealing with.

'It's your fault. You're irresistible.'

He kissed her again, softly, lingering, wondering how he'd ever had the will power to turn this amazing woman down all those years ago and wondering what the hell he was going to do when she walked out of his life this time around.

She had his libido firing on all cylinders but it was more than that. They'd reconnected on so many levels, their special friendship a thing to be treasured.

But what had changed?

Career-driven Brittany Lloyd would hightail it out of Noosa without a backward glance, leaving him cursing the day he'd been foolish enough to let her back into his heart, a heart he'd deliberately closed off from ever loving any woman too much.

He might've obliterated memories of his mum but he'd never forgotten the pain of abandonment, the intense loss that had clawed at his insides, the doubts that had plagued him for years that he wasn't good enough to be loved for ever.

'How irresistible?'

Now wasn't a time for doubts or deliberating or questioning as he kissed her again, deepened the kiss, craving intimacy as the parched outback craved water to sustain life. The thought of losing her did it, prompting him to do all manner of crazy things like back her up against the table, wishing he'd had the sense to lock the back door.

Her hands dived into his hair, angling his head for better access to his mouth as she wrapped a leg around his waist, bringing him into delicious contact with her heat, and blind, raging need slammed through him to the point of no return.

He was out of his mind with need for her but he'd be damned if he took her standing up against a kitchen wall after all this time.

She deserved more.

She deserved the universe and then some.

Wrenching his mouth from hers with effort, he exhaled on a long, ragged breath as he broke the full-length body contact he'd been relishing so much.

'Nick?'

'Not now, not here, not like this,' he said through gritted teeth, desperate to rein in his libido as he tried not to focus on her swollen mouth, on the lips he'd tasted, lips he'd savoured, lips he'd kiss all night long if he had his way.

'Then when?'

Confusion clouded her eyes as he balled his hands to stop from hauling her back into his arms, silently cursed making a hash of this.

Desire pounded through his veins, untamed and undisciplined and uncontrollable, but he'd subdue his ferocious need for now, bide his time, for when they gave into this tempestuous passion he would stop at nothing less than making love to her all night long.

With great restraint he settled for trailing a fingertip down her cheek, along her jaw, enjoying the instant flare of heat in her sparkling eyes, the soft little smile playing about her lips.

He cupped her chin, his gaze not leaving hers. 'Soon, Red. Very soon.'

Something fierce, something wild and something altogether terrifying flashed across her face before she nodded, slowly.

'Good,' she breathed on a sigh, setting his heart pumping with wild anticipation as he grabbed her hand and almost dragged her out of the door before he changed his mind.

Brittany hadn't had this much fun in ages.

Sure, she attended swank parties in London and rubbed shoulders with the rich and famous thanks to her brilliant job, but those events were filled with pretentious flakes who spoke to you depending on which designer dressed you or how many millions you made a year.

She hated the way money talked, hated the way it divided people into classes and, while she understood Nick's drive to gain acceptance into the privileged world she'd been born into for the sake of his business, she couldn't help but wish he'd wanted to marry her for her all those years ago.

They'd both changed so much, yet when he touched her, when he kissed her, the last decade vanished on a wistful sigh.

They'd been too young back then; she could see it now. She'd romanticised what they had, had mistaken the throes of first love as being something to build a lifetime commitment on.

But Nick hadn't been ready and, while his deliberate sabotaging of their relationship at the end had hurt, she understood.

His father had meant everything to him while she hadn't been able to wait to escape hers. They'd had different dreams at the time, different goals.

So where did that leave them now?

Could two successful, career-driven people take a chance on love?

She collapsed onto a portable chair in a corner of the harvesting shed, her gaze homing in on Nick surrounded by a bunch of investors while images of the scintillating kiss they'd shared in the kitchen a few hours earlier replayed over and over, making her shiver anew.

That had been some kiss. Passionate, mind-blowing and way too intense, the type of kiss to pin hopes on, the type of kiss to give a girl ideas of how he felt. And on the heels of his admission on their wedding night, when he'd said he cared about her, way too baffling.

She'd been trying to tempt him, trying to seduce him, but he'd had nerves of steel.

Until tonight.

That kiss in the kitchen had changed everything.

He wanted her as much as she wanted him, so why had he stopped? Pulled away?

Damn, the man was infuriating and confusing the heck out of her.

Every time he touched her, she lost it. But that didn't mean she had to lose her head completely.

Having fun and walking away was one thing.

Having fun and falling for him another.

No. This time, she'd be smarter than that. She'd come too far from the scared, confused teenager who'd bolted like a fugitive into the night to regress.

She didn't need anyone. She'd been doing fine on her own for the last ten years, thank you very much, and getting involved emotionally with Nick would only lead to heartache for them both.

'Hey, what's with the look?' Frida Rutger, Bram's much younger trophy wife, flopped into a chair next to her and fanned her face. 'Is it hot in here or what?'

'Sure is.'

Brittany deliberately ignored Frida's first question, glad for the interruption; anything to distract from her thoughts of Nick.

However, she should've known the astute young woman who'd hosted parties for world dignitaries wouldn't let her off that easily.

'So, why the glum look? Has that dishy new husband of yours done something to upset you?'

'No.'

Unless she counted upsetting her equilibrium. 'Just tired, I guess.'

Frida's gaze bordered on jealous as it zeroed in on Nick. 'I'm not surprised, married to someone like that.'

Uncomfortable with the woman's frank admiration—and shocked by the urge to scratch her eyes out—Brittany aimed for distraction.

'Your dress is gorgeous. Local designer?'

Thankfully, Frida's greedy gaze abandoned Nick and focused on her stunning ochre and crimson layered chiffon dress, the bodice hugging her fake boobs until it reached her waist, where it cascaded in a fiery waterfall of riotous colour to her ankles.

'I designed it myself.'

The thought of the wife of Queensland's richest man making her own dress almost shocked her as much as Nick's unexpected kiss earlier.

'Wow, you're a talented designer.'

To her horror, Frida's bottom lip wobbled as she blinked frantically. 'Pity Bram doesn't think so.' She sniffed, plucked at a chiffon layer in her lap. 'He said it looked like a bottle of orange soda exploded all over me.'

Brittany watched Bram, paunchy and balding and florid-faced, slap Nick on the back, while his beautiful wife fought tears.

Searching for a diplomatic answer, she finally said,

'Bram's a great businessman, but maybe his fashion sense isn't up to par?'

Frida dashed her tears away with an angry swipe, a smile twitching at her mouth.

'He also said I need liposuction and another facelift.'

Outraged, she abandoned all sense of politeness. 'Guys are jerks.'

However, when her gaze returned to Nick, drawn by the magnetic power he exuded by just being in a room, she knew her statement wasn't entirely true. Not all guys...

'You can say that again.'

'Guys are jerks.'

Frida chuckled and she joined in, wondering how an attractive young woman could hook up with an overbearing ass like Bram.

It all came down to money and, once again, she thanked her lucky stars she'd escaped that world and all it stood for.

'Aren't you the lucky one? Here comes your delicious husband.' Frida jumped up and smoothed her dress, tears forgotten as she batted her eyelashes at Nick. 'Nice to see you, Nick.'

Nick nodded, his gaze fixed on Brittany rather than the eye-catching figure sashaying away in a fiery dress, earning him more Brownie points than she could count.

He sat beside her, his aftershave teasing her to lean closer, to fill her senses with it, as she had earlier when she'd lost herself in the wonder of his kiss.

'I don't like it when women natter in corners. They're usually planning trouble for us mere males.'

His frown didn't work when accompanied by a slow, sexy smile that notched up the heat between them in a second.

'Safety in numbers, I guess.'

Leaning towards her, he crooked his finger. 'Looks to me like numbers are dwindling, and you know what that means?'

'What?'

He sent her an exaggerated wink. 'It means we'll have to spike the band's drinks so we get rid of the rest of the revellers pronto.'

She laughed while her heart stopped its jumping around and settled with a resounding thud.

For at that moment, she knew.

His promised 'soon' had arrived and with his bow tie askew, his dark hair rumpled and light brown eyes blazing with an emotion she daredn't analyse, she had as much chance of not falling in love with Nick again as flying solo back to London.

And the knowledge he still held that kind of power over her scared her beyond belief.

'How much longer?'

She needed him to hold her, to erase her thoughts, to banish the yearning to be with him for ever. Surely they would make love tonight, would assuage the tension strumming between them? 'Soon' couldn't come quick enough as far as she was concerned.

Sensing her eagerness, he slid an arm around her waist and cuddled her close.

'I'll get the band to announce this is the final number. How's that?'

'Perfect.'

'Don't move. I'll be right back.'

Feathering a kiss across her lips, he strode away, leaving her to deal with her newly awakened feelings and how much they terrified her.

The time would come shortly for her to sort them out and she wasn't looking forward to the wake-up call she knew was inevitable when she had to leave, not one bit.

CHAPTER TEN

BRITTANY paced the kitchen, waiting for Nick to see the last reveller off the property.

She shouldn't be this nervous.

It wasn't as if she'd never made love to him before.

Though as she watched him stride towards the house, broad shoulders squared, long legs eating up the distance, a full moon casting shadows across his face and glinting in his dark hair, she knew the man he was today was a far cry from the boy he'd been ten years earlier.

If she'd loved that Nick unreservedly, unashamedly and unabashedly, what hope did she have of holding back her emotions this time around?

As he neared the door she quickly dropped into the nearest chair and picked up a magazine from a messy stack in the corner, pretending to flip through it without a care in the world.

When he entered, she took a peek over the top of the magazine, confused by his wide grin.

'Everyone gone?'

So much for casual. Her voice came out a high-pitched squeak and she cleared her throat, rustling the magazine, ready to duck behind it.

'Uh-huh.'

He stalked towards her and she gulped, wanting to be in his arms so much it hurt, yet petrified once she was there she'd never want to leave.

'A bit of light reading?'

'Mmm.'

His muffled guffaw said he hadn't bought her ruse for a second. 'That's interesting. I'd never have pegged you for a girl interested in cattle mating seasons.'

Heat swept her cheeks as she slapped the pages shut, flung the magazine back on the pile and folded her arms.

'Because if you are, you can have those magazines. They were Papa's and I'm in the process of doing a major clean-out before the sale, so be my guest.'

Seeing the funny side of it, she shook her head. 'Thanks, but I'll pass. Leave the cows and bulls to it.'

The twinkle in his eyes intensified as he held out a hand to her and gently pulled her to her feet. 'You know, you don't have to be nervous around me.'

'I'm not.'

A quick rebuttal easily belied by her tumbling belly and wobbly knees and hands that shook ever so slightly.

He sent a pointed glance at the magazine and raised an eyebrow. 'Really?'

She sighed, placed her palms on his chest to anchor her before she wobbled any more and embarrassed herself further.

'Okay, okay, I'm a tad nervous. Aren't you?'

'No.'

He slid his arms around her waist, creating a welcoming cocoon she could quite happily snuggle in for ever.

'We're not strangers. This is you and me, Red.'

'But—'

'No buts. Unless it involves this one.'

He gave her backside a playful pinch and she laughed, her nerves dissipating as he'd intended.

'Tonight is about you and me. No second guessing. No overanalysing. No regrets. Okay?'

It all sounded very logical when he put it like that, but she knew come morning she'd be analysing every single second.

She'd always been this way around him, off course and off kilter, and now the moment she'd been anticipating had arrived she couldn't quell the bundle of nerves knotting her resolve.

She wanted him. It should be simple, right?

But nothing was simple about her relationship with this dynamic, enigmatic man and the moment she started under-estimating the power of his hold over her was the moment she'd lose control.

Not a bad thing entirely, but she was scared, terrified in fact, by the depth of emotion for a bad-boy rebel who still cradled her heart in his powerful hands.

'You're thinking too much.'

She nodded, her mouth kicking up in a wry grin. He knew her so well, knew she'd be analysing every angle of this momentous step.

'Well, I'm done thinking.'

Before she could blink he covered her mouth with his, his commanding kiss obliterating every doubt, every thought, she'd just had.

As his tongue duelled with hers she lost herself in the mindless passion instantly ignited between them, the frantic flurry of eager hands and low moans and hot, bare skin.

'I didn't want it to be like this, not here—'

'Don't stop,' she panted, arching into him, her pelvis melding to his, so hard and ready. 'Please, Nick, now.'

His low, guttural groan raised goose bumps along her skin as his hands bunched her skirt up around her thighs while he plundered her mouth again.

Sensation after sensation bombarded her, from his mouth

ravaging hers with fierce intent to his hands stroking her thighs and brushing against her mound.

Endless, mindless pleasure, which built and receded and built again until she could barely stand any more and when his fingers finally delved beneath the elastic of her thong and circled her clitoris she came apart on a long, drawn-out cry.

'Nick, that was—'

'Just the beginning.'

His wicked grin sent a tremor of excitement through her sated body and she gasped when he spun her around, his arm pinning her waist, her back in delicious contact with his front. His very aroused front.

'Let me please you—'

'You already have, sweetheart, by hearing you come,' he whispered in her ear, his teeth grazing the lobe, nipping, nuzzling until she could do little but sag against him, boneless with longing and pleasure. 'But just so you know, I'm calling the shots now.'

'Ah…my forceful bad boy is back.'

With a faux growl, he hugged her tighter. 'Then it's time I showed you just how bad I can be.'

Her body shuddered as he slid his hands up her ribcage to cradle her breasts, his thumbs teasing her nipples until a veritable flood of mind-numbing need drenched her.

He didn't stop there, oh, no, making good on his promise of being 'bad' as one hand braced the wall over her shoulder while the other played over her wet core.

Desire tightened within her, her hips rocking of their own volition as her inner muscles spasmed again and again as she threw back her head in absolute abandonment.

'Nick…'

She cried out his name as a part-plea, part-warning; she couldn't take much more of this, needed him inside her now.

'I'm right here.'

With a swift rip of unzipping metal and a rustle of tearing foil, he was back, pushing against her, holding her hips and angling them forward as he nudged against her entrance.

'Nick, please…'

He drove into her, hard and fast and heart-stoppingly long, the exquisite pressure filling her, tantalising her.

She'd waited so long for this, had dreamed about it, and when he started to pull out and thrust back into her, again and again and again, the sheer intense beauty of it robbed her of breath, of reason.

'Britt, my Britt.'

His possessiveness thrilled her as much as his hands gripping her hips, tilting them to increase the tempting friction as he plunged into her repeatedly, his rhythm driving them both towards a shattering climax.

'Wow,' she breathed on a sigh, her entire body humming and thrumming and sated as she sagged against him, her head lolling against his shoulder.

His barely audible oath had her head jerking up as she spun around to face him. 'What's wrong?'

'This. Here.'

He gestured around the kitchen before dropping his gaze to her bunched skirt and thong around her knees, shaking his head. 'You deserve more than this.'

Mustering what little dignity a woman with her knickers around her knees could have, she wriggled back into her thong before jabbing him in the chest.

'Don't you dare apologise for the best sex I've ever had. It was perfect. Better than perfect, it was stupendous.'

The corners of his wickedly sexy mouth kicked up. 'The best, huh?'

She nodded emphatically. 'The best.'

His grin widened. 'So you like a guy so out of control he can't make it to the bedroom?'

Grabbing his lapels, she hauled him close until their noses almost touched.

'Not just any guy, I like you, Nick Mancini. Every delicious bad-boy inch of you.'

'I love it when you talk dirty to me.'

'I didn't mean—'

'I know.'

He chuckled, rubbed noses with her as he stroked her back, long, languid strokes that relaxed her, and she rested her cheek on his chest, inhaling his seductive scent.

'Do you think it's ironic we're back here where it all started?'

She pulled away, glanced up at him. 'You mean my first time?'

He nodded, caressed her cheek with a tenderness that stole her breath and warmed her heart.

'I wanted to make it special for you then too. So what happened? The oven was on the blink so the pizza was cold, the dessert wouldn't defrost and I sprayed cola all over you.'

She smiled at the memories. 'That night was special, and it was all because of you.'

Her fingertips skimmed his jaw, savouring the faint prickle of stubble before hovering over his lips, tracing their outline. 'You were incredible, and I've never forgotten that night.'

Or the few months after it, when they'd sneak down to the river to make love underneath the towering eucalypts or beneath the beautiful jacarandas.

To this day, she couldn't walk past a jacaranda without blushing, its unique fragrance a poignant reminder of Nick laying her on a carpet of purple blossoms and taking her to the heavens and back.

'I say we recreate the magic. Though this time, we might even make it to the bedroom. You in?'

Excitement trickled through her body, fast becoming a raging torrent as she nodded and he swept her into his arms and headed for his old bedroom.

'I'm definitely in,' she said, laughing out loud when he twirled her around a few times before bumping the door open with his hip.

'Good, because if you'd said no I would've dropped you.'

Nipping the skin beneath his jaw, she nuzzled him. 'You wouldn't dare.'

'Never dare a rebel,' he said, dumping her on the bed before joining her, their laughter surrounding them in lovely warmth.

'Oh, wow.'

She glanced around the room, at the wooden shelves stacked high with trophies, several motorbike helmets in one corner, old leather jackets in the other.

'This room hasn't changed.'

He shrugged, somewhat embarrassed. 'I never stay out here. My life's in Noosa now. I guess Papa was too busy running the place when he was alive to worry about changing the bedrooms.'

Did he know his voice changed when he spoke of his father? Deepened? Softened? As if caught up in good times.

She envied him that, had always envied him the easy, close relationship he'd shared with his dad. It was one of the reasons she'd liked hanging out here so much; that and the mean lasagne Papa used to cook.

'I love this place. Do you really need to sell?'

A momentary shadow clouded his eyes before he blinked and it vanished.

'It's not fair to let it run down. And I just don't have the time to do much out here.'

'Why don't you hire a manager? Farm hands? Get the plantation up and running again?'

He shook his head, the tiny indentation between his brows a sign she was butting into business that was no concern of hers.

'You know what this place meant to Papa.'

He didn't have to add 'and to me'. She could see his reluctance to sell in his clenched jaw, in his rigid neck muscles, could hear it in his tense tone.

'All the more reason to keep it, bring it back to life—'

'It's time to let the place go. You of all people should understand the power of memories and the need to move on from the past.'

Oh, yeah, she understood the need to move on all too well. As for memories, her good ones were all focused on Nick and, rather than push the issue about the farm, she needed to start creating new ones.

'Yeah, I get it.' Her gaze caught a flash of silver hanging off the mirror. 'Hey, is that the medallion I gave you?'

He followed her line of vision, the slight pink staining his tanned cheeks a dead giveaway he'd rather forget the fact he'd kept a girly trinket.

'Maybe.'

She rolled off the bed, evading his arms as he made a lunge for her.

'It is! I can't believe you kept it all this time.'

'Like I said, this room has been untouched since I left it.'

Her heart expanded as she slung the delicate chain on her finger, tracing the outline of the star on the medallion with her finger.

'You know why I chose a star, don't you?'

He shook his head and she dangled the chain on her finger a second longer before rehanging it on the mirror.

'Because you hung the stars and moon for me back then.'

He came up behind her, slid his arms around her waist and held her close.

'And now?'

'Let's find out.'

She turned in the circle of his embrace, ready for his kiss, every cell in her body crying out for him, only him.

His mouth moved over hers, hot, challenging, and she matched him, their kisses deep and long and luscious, the type of kisses to melt a body and sear a soul.

If they'd kissed like this all night long she would've been happy, but she didn't want to settle. Not tonight.

Tonight she wanted those stars and that moon.

'I want you so much,' he murmured, trailing his lips down her neck as his thumbs nudged the underside of her breasts, toying with her, teasing her, before drifting upwards to circle her tight nipples through the silk.

Her head fell back on a moan as he deftly flicked the clasp on her shoulder and the Grecian dress slithered down her body in a rustle of silk, its caress almost as erotic as Nick's hands.

'Jeez,' he muttered, his gaze raking her from head to foot before resting on her breasts, the naked need in his eyes sending a tremor of unbridled lust shooting through her. 'You're even more gorgeous now, if that's possible.'

Smiling, she tugged on his jacket. 'Still the sweet talker.'

He shook his head, his dazed expression vindication he found her mature body just as appealing as the lithe teenager she'd once been.

Sliding the jacket off his shoulders, she started working on his bow tie. 'But for now, less talk, more action.'

'You want to see some action?'

His scorching kiss had her grateful for the edge of the bed bumping the backs of her knees as she collapsed onto it, happily watching as he shucked off the rest of his clothes in record time.

'I like those,' she said, pointing to the black boxers that had been haunting her dreams ever since she'd glimpsed them on their wedding night.

'And I like those.'

He toyed with the top of her white lace thong, sending a river of heat straight to her core.

'But not enough to keep them on.'

He whipped them off and tossed them over his shoulder, his eyes glazing as his gaze roamed her.

'Come here.'

She held her arms out to him and he entered her embrace in a second, the touch of his bare skin against hers sizzling hot.

He kissed her, laved her, delved his fingers into her until she was panting for release, clutching at him, crying out his name, sobbing her need when the mind-numbing tension climbed and spiralled and shattered into a million shooting stars.

She couldn't think, couldn't speak, and she whimpered when he left her for a moment to rip off his boxers and roll a condom on.

'I'm right here, sweetheart.'

'Where you belong,' she said, a second before his mouth claimed hers and he lay on top of her, sliding inside with a smooth, powerful thrust that made her gasp.

He filled her, completed her and she wrapped her legs around him, tilting her hips to encourage deeper contact.

Then he moved, sliding in and out, every move sending shards of exquisite pleasure firing through her, making every nerve ending sit up and cry for more.

And he gave her more.

He drove into her, his chest rasping her sensitised nipples, his tongue mating with hers, his rhythm taking them higher and higher until he stiffened and cried out her name, shuddering into her.

Brittany had no idea how long they stayed locked together, their heart rates slowly calming, their breathing soft and ragged.

She didn't mind his weight, didn't mind the slick of sweat between their bodies.

She'd asked for the stars and the moon.

Nick had delivered the whole damn solar system.

CHAPTER ELEVEN

SLEEPING with Britt had been a bad idea.

Not that there'd been much sleeping involved.

Their cataclysmic night had changed everything.

'This place hasn't changed a bit,' she said, tugging his hand as she ran towards the river's edge, leaving Nick no option but to follow.

And follow he would, to the ends of the earth if she asked, for last night had shattered any illusions he had about this marriage being all business.

With every kiss, with every caress, with every gut-wrenching moan, she'd stripped away the years, catapulting him straight back to a time he was so crazy for her he couldn't see straight.

Nothing had changed, absolutely nothing.

Even that was a lie.

Ten years ago, he'd been a fool, kidding himself all he felt for Britt was lust.

Now he knew the truth.

What they'd shared had never just been about lust; it was more than that, so much more.

And their night of passion had hurtled him back a decade, to a time he couldn't get enough of her, to a time where his heart clamoured towards her while his head reeled back with the implications of trusting a woman.

'Do you miss Jacaranda?'

She stopped, alerted to the seriousness of his question by something in his voice as he waved towards the river, trying to distract her.

It didn't work, for she reached up, cupped his cheek, her simple touch as catastrophic as if she'd reached into his chest and squeezed his heart.

'I tried not to. I tried to forget.'

Her fingertips trailed down his cheek, lingered on his jaw, before dropping lower where she placed her palm flat against his chest, directly over his heart. Claiming ownership. It was hers, had always been hers, he just never admitted it.

'But I couldn't. This place is in my blood. I never forgot it.'

She paused, massaged his chest gently as if soothing his soul. 'I never forgot you.'

'Same here.'

He settled his mouth over hers, needing this kiss, aching for it. Nothing like the ache of how he'd wanted her last night, when he'd been blinded by lust and passion.

Uh-uh, this ache settled right over his heart, exactly where her hand was, the kind of ache that scared the hell out of him.

Her lips parted, so soft, so moist, and he groaned as his tongue touched hers, going a little crazy as he backed her up against the nearest tree, their bodies melding perfectly, his hands sliding under her top, cupping her breasts.

'Nick…'

Her wanton plea made his hard-on throb as he lifted her top, ducked his head, and captured an erect nipple between his teeth, plucking at the lace covering it, her low moans firing him to flick the clasp and allow the tempting lushness to fall into his hands.

But the Jacaranda fauna had other ideas as a raucous cackle of a nearby kookaburra pierced the silence and reminded him of where they were.

In the good old days this river bed was deserted but now the worn track along the bank showed exactly how popular this spot was with bushwalkers and tourists and he had no intention of providing an X-rated show for any of them.

Reluctantly tugging her top down, he brushed a soft kiss against her lips.

'You used to love those damn birds. Too bad this one has shocking timing.'

She laughed, a clear, joyous sound that had him chuckling right along with her. 'Remember the time we made out down here and—?'

'Can we change the subject?' He sent a pointed look at his groin. 'You're killing me, in case you hadn't noticed.'

As she ground her pelvis against his her smile was pure evil. 'Oh, I noticed.'

She slid her hands around his neck, bringing her breasts flush against his chest. 'Why don't we continue this *discussion* back at the farm?'

'You're one wicked woman,' he said, smoothing stray tendrils of copper gold away from her face, his heart bucking at the adoration in her eyes.

He wanted her to look at him like this, wanted her. Then why the faintest doubt he was deluding himself, about everything?

One night and he'd been blinded to the transient nature of their marriage: her job, her promotion, their deal.

Last night changed everything, but they hadn't discussed it, any of it, and while now wasn't ideal there would come a time soon, very soon, where they'd both need to lay it all on the line.

'Come on, let's head back.'

He didn't need to be asked twice and as they sprinted back to the farmhouse, laughing and falling over their flying feet, he banished his doubts and decided to live in the moment.

For now.

* * *

Brittany paced from one end of their suite to the other, casting malevolent glances at her laptop on each circuit and the incriminating email on the screen.

The promotion was hers.

David had seen the preliminary pitch she'd emailed, blown away by the video footage, pictures of the plantation and the accompanying spread, had evaluated it and made his decision.

She was the new managing director of Sell.

She'd done it.

Which meant her work here was done.

So where did that leave her and Nick?

She should be ecstatic, her dream finally a reality with the added bonus of clearing her debt to Daddy dearest and finally being free of her past.

Instead, dread warred with terror as she mentally rehearsed her spiel.

She had to tell Nick the truth.

She was leaving, heading back to her job, back to a dream she'd worked incredibly hard for, had strived for, had given up a heck of a lot for.

But what if the dream had changed?

What if the dream had evolved to include a sexy billionaire, a pristine beach and a very real marriage?

At the sound of the door opening she stopped, lunged at the laptop and slammed it shut.

She was nowhere near ready for this.

'Hey, how's the most beautiful girl in Noosa doing?'

'Great.'

She forced a smile, quelling the urge to blurt the truth the instant he stepped through the door.

He opened his arms. 'Come here. Rough day at the office and I need a welcome kiss from my wife.'

She flew into his arms, crushing her lips to his in an urgent, validating kiss before burrowing into his chest, seeking comfort, seeking warmth, seeking a solution to her terrible dilemma.

She wanted the promotion.

She wanted him.

And never the twain should meet.

'What's up?'

He pulled away, his hands spanning her waist, anchoring her in a world spinning dangerously out of control.

'We need to discuss our arrangement.'

Frowning, he dropped his hands and stepped away, leaving her cursing her choice of words and wishing there were a simple solution to this.

But there wasn't and she needed to face the truth: she'd fallen for Nick all over again, had blown her 'have fun for a short time not a long time' motto and, in doing so, had the potential to blow her dream job too.

'By arrangement I assume you mean our marriage?'

She nodded, biting her bottom lip as his face wiped of all expression, his cool indifference a frightening reminder of the emotional barriers he'd slammed up the weeks leading up to the night he'd dashed her dreams of a future ten years earlier.

'I got the promotion.'

'Congratulations.'

He thrust his hands in his pockets, his calculating gaze not leaving hers, as if daring her to continue, daring her to speak her mind and put an end to this.

'It's all happened rather soon—'

'When do you leave?'

No begging her to stay, no declaration of undying love.

But then, what did she expect?

Ever since their marriage had turned physical they'd slipped into old ways; comfortable with each other, teasing, joking, making up for lost time in the bedroom.

Yet they'd skirted around the issue of a future, never

chatting beyond the day-to-day events, making love with frantic abandon as if each time could be their last.

It reminded her of the past, of the fragile nature of their relationship back then. But Nick wasn't the bad-ass rebel any more and she wasn't the wide-eyed romantic dreaming of happily ever after.

She hadn't got as far as she had in her career without being practical and there was no way she'd give up on them without a fight.

There had to be a solution to this, there just had to be.

Grabbing her hair and twisting it into a loose knot at the base of her neck, she sank onto the edge of the bed and patted it.

'My leaving depends on you.'

He eyed her warily, his rigid posture at odds with the fleeting yearning in his eyes as his gaze strayed to the spot next to her.

'Come on, take a seat. We need to sort this out.'

'Fine.'

With a terse nod, he flung himself into an armchair opposite, his inflexible expression not giving an inch.

'Don't trust me?'

'Don't trust myself.'

A glimmer of a smile tugged at the corners of his mouth, giving her hope. 'You know what happens any time I get near you on a bed.'

'Not just a bed, from memory.'

His eyes darkened to burnt caramel and she swallowed. It was so easy slipping into old ways with him; teasing, flirting. But flirting wouldn't solve this, nothing but a good dose of honesty would, and she steadied her resolve to confront this rather than tumble into bed with him and forget everything.

She shook her head, breaking eye contact, and when she met his gaze again he'd cooled, slipping those darn barriers firmly back in place.

'What do you want?'

The million-dollar question: if only she had a priceless answer.

'Honestly? I want it all. My job, the promotion, you…'

She trailed off, hoping he'd fill the void, say something, anything, to give her some indication he wanted this marriage to work as much as she did.

But he didn't move, didn't speak, his lips clamped shut in tight disapproval, leaving her floundering for her next words when she was usually brilliantly articulate at work.

With her job, she knew what she wanted and knew what to say to get it. She'd nailed pitches other companies craved, had climbed to the top with sheer determination.

Those skills weren't exclusive to advertising and right now she knew what she wanted, and he was staring at her with studied apathy she knew had to be a front.

'I know this marriage was a business arrangement at first, but the boundaries have changed.'

Taking a deep breath, she made the pitch of her life. 'I want this marriage to work, and not just because of our deal at the start. We've got something special, something that time apart hasn't erased, and I know if we give this a chance it can be the best thing to happen to us.'

His expression thawed, his shoulders relaxing as he swiped a hand over his face and she went for broke.

'Whatever it takes to make this marriage work, I'll do it. If it means giving up my job in London and moving here…'

She shrugged, shocked by the words coming out of her mouth, yet strangely relieved.

She'd voiced a solution, a terrifying, monstrous, life-changing solution, and rather than being overwhelmed by the enormity of it her heart expanded, filled with a surprising peace.

Shock darkened his eyes to chocolate as he leaned forward, bracing his elbows on his knees.

'You'd do that for me?'

'For us.'

Padding over to join him, she plopped onto his lap, leaving him no option but to hold her.

'Hell, Red, I don't know what to say.'

'Then don't say anything for now.'

She placed a finger against his lips, yearning to trace the contours but knowing this wasn't the time. Despite his shell-shocked expression he hadn't lost the wariness and she knew he needed time: time to think, to assimilate, to decide.

She knew what she wanted; it looked as if her husband needed to figure out the same.

'Think about it. We'll talk later.'

Brushing a kiss across his lips, she slipped from his arms, saddened he let her go but determined to give him the time he needed.

She'd done her bit to save their marriage.

The rest was up to him.

CHAPTER TWELVE

NICK did the one thing guaranteed to blow away the cobwebs of confusion threading his thoughts into a muddled jumble.

He hit the road.

Slamming his visor down, he glanced over his shoulder, let out the throttle and savoured the roar of the motorbike as he pulled out onto the open highway.

It had been way too long since he'd done this.

Putting his past behind him came at a price and, while slaving his guts out to make a success of his business had worked, he missed the simple things in life. Like making pasta from scratch, cooking the rich, creamy sauces Papa had shown him, growing the herbs to complete any good Italian meal, taking off on a whim and riding as far as a tank of petrol lasted.

And Britt.

He'd missed her more than he'd ever imagined, hadn't known how much until she'd strutted back into his life with her fancy suits and stellar career.

The simple life...he'd had it once but had moved on. For what? Fame? Fortune? To impress a bunch of rich phoneys who hadn't given him the time of day until he'd proven he could be responsible by marrying?

He'd been a fool.

None of it mattered, not any more.

Britt wanted him.

At what cost? He couldn't let her give up her dream for him and, as much as he appreciated how far she was willing to go to give them a chance, it scared the hell out of him.

They'd barely been married six weeks and she was willing to lay it all on the line? For him?

Old doubts crept under his guard, crawled under his skin until he itched to pull over and scratch them away.

What if he wasn't good enough for her?

What if he couldn't be the man she deserved?

What if she didn't need him as much as he needed her?

Yeah, the same old doubts, undermining the confident, successful man he'd become.

Crazy. But then, so was their unrelenting passion that hadn't waned in ten long years.

But were they making up for lost time? Fulfilling an affair they never really had first time around? Confusing a sizzling attraction for a deeper emotion they'd need as a solid foundation to build a real marriage on?

The wind filled his ears, not loud enough to obliterate the questions whirling through his head, and he glanced down at the speedometer, muttering a curse as he realised he'd momentarily lost concentration.

All this mulling was pointless anyway. Until he cleared the past, he couldn't make way for the future.

If they were to have any future, he had to tell Britt the truth. All of it.

Making an impulsive decision that had landed him in more scrapes as a youngster than he cared to admit, he slowed, checked for traffic and made a U-turn.

Time to pay his past a visit.

Nick rang the reception bell, glancing around as he waited. He'd assumed the local special accommodation for the elderly

would be shabby, run-down, with the cloying smell of disin-
fectant and overcooked stew in the air.

Surprisingly, this place could pass for a hotel with its mani-
cured lawns, new whitewash, elegant furniture and sweeping
veranda, with floor-to-ceiling windows highlighting a breathtaking vista. Then again, would he expect Darby Lloyd to live
in anything less?

'Can I help you?'

A middle-aged woman in a nurse's uniform bustled out from
a back room and leaned over the desk with a beaming smile.

'I hope so. I'd like to see Darby Lloyd?'

To her credit, the nurse's smile didn't slip, but he saw the
fleeting surprise in her twinkling eyes.

'Certainly. Darby doesn't get many visitors so I'm sure
he'll be thrilled to see you.'

He bit back a grin. The last thing good old Darby would
be was thrilled.

'Follow me.'

If the outside had been impressive, the inside of the place
knocked him for six as he followed the nurse down a series
of corridors. Paintings of every size and description covered
the walls, antiques tastefully arranged on every available inch
of furniture and the rich, polished Tasmanian Oak floorboards
gleamed in the late afternoon light pouring through the
atrium-like ceilings.

The nurse came to an abrupt halt outside a mahogany door
and gestured him forward. 'Just knock and head on in. Though
please keep your visit brief. Darby's blood pressure's elevated
and he has a tendency to overdo things.'

'You have my word.'

His wink was rewarded with a blush and a smile as she
bustled away, leaving him with lead in his boots.

He shouldn't have come here, unannounced, especially if
the old man was having a bad day. He hadn't seen Darby in

ten years, hadn't wanted to after what he'd done, but that was the past and if he wanted to move forward he had to lay it to rest, once and for all.

He took a deep breath, knocked twice and pushed the door open.

'Mr Lloyd, it's Nick Mancini.'

He'd hated this man for years, had mentally prepared himself to face his nemesis. What he hadn't prepared for was the swift rush of compassion for the pale, frail old man sitting in a recliner, propped up by a mountain of pillows, his eyes closed.

He'd never seen Darby anything but overbearing, arrogant and mean, lording his wealth over everyone foolish enough to get close to him and anyone else who crossed his path. But that man had disappeared beneath a plethora of wrinkles and a greyish pallor that suggested a long-standing illness.

Anxious to get this over and done with, Nick cleared his throat and stepped into the room.

'What the hell are you doing here?'

Darby's eyes flew open, their feverish glint a startling contrast to the pallor of his pasty skin.

'We need to talk, clear the air.'

'I've got nothing to say to you, so get out.'

Still the same cantankerous fool, but there was no way he was leaving without saying his piece.

'I will, but before I go you need to listen.'

Nick kept his voice devoid of emotion, not wanting to agitate the old guy further considering he'd now flushed an ugly crimson.

'About you marrying my daughter? About bringing disgrace on this family? Dragging our name through the mud?' Darby sat bolt upright, shook a fist at him. 'I don't want to hear it. You've won, damn you. Isn't that enough?'

Clenching his fists, Nick shoved them deep into his jacket

pockets, not willing to show the slightest indication he felt anything other than indifference for Darby's poisonous barbs.

Before he could utter a word, Darby pushed up from his chair, his neck muscles rigid, his expression thunderous, his eyes gleaming with a maniacal edge.

'Just because I'm stuck in this godforsaken place don't think I'm stupid, boy. I know what you're up to, marrying Brittany out of spite, taking your revenge on me.' He stabbed his finger in the air, tottering slightly. 'That stupid girl deserves everything she gets for running around with the likes of you. She won't get another penny out of me now. I've given her more than enough to pad her new life in London. So if you were hoping for a silver lining to your marriage, too bad. You can both go to the devil.'

Nick silently swore and took a step back, not wanting to believe what he was hearing but, like onlookers at an accident, drawn to the horrifying carnage.

The extent of Darby Lloyd's hatred didn't shock him half as much as his total disregard for his only child, and if the old guy didn't look as if he had one foot in the grave, Nick would willingly give him a shove in that direction for his callousness towards Britt.

Instilling a calm he knew would drive the old coot mad, he said, 'You're wrong. Our marriage has nothing to do with you or what happened in the past. She's your daughter. Don't you care enough about her to at least maintain civilities with me?'

Darby flushed puce, staggered and flopped back in his chair while Nick shook his head.

He'd been wrong to come here.

Time hadn't soothed the old man's rampant prejudice; it had festered and grown until he couldn't see reason.

'Get out, Mancini, and don't come back.'

Shaking his head, Nick opened the door. By the old guy's shallow breaths and mottled red cheeks, he should probably send the nurse in before he left.

'One more thing, Mancini.'

He paused on the threshold, turned, eager to get out of this place and back to Britt. He could tell her all of it now, for nothing either of them could say or do would make an ounce of difference where Darby was concerned.

'Yeah?'

'I hope you rot in hell for going near my daughter in the first place.'

Without a word, Nick walked out and didn't look back.

Brittany reread the same paragraph for the fifth time before leaping up from the keyboard.

Work had succeeded in distracting her from losing Nick a decade earlier, but it wasn't doing a thing for her now. She'd scanned her emails, managed to form coherent replies for the important ones, read the documentation David had forwarded from Human Resources and toyed with an idea to grab the lucrative advertising contract for a World Cup soccer team.

All perfectly stimulating stuff she would normally thrive on, but today she couldn't concentrate for more than a few seconds at a time, her mind constantly drifting to Nick.

Where was he?

What was he thinking?

Why had he run out on her when they needed to discuss this like two normal people?

He needed time, she understood. But the fact he'd barely spoken more than two syllables since she'd dropped her bombshell didn't bode well.

Bombshell? She'd detonated their relationship clean out of the water; first, with the news she was leaving, then with her follow-up declaration she'd give up her dream job to be with her dream man.

Was she crazy?

Yeah, crazy about a bad-boy billionaire with molten-toffee eyes and a smile that made her belly clench with desire.

Heading for the window where she could waste another half-hour or so staring at the killer view without really seeing it, she stopped as she heard the door open and swung around in time to see Nick burst into the suite, his hair dishevelled, his expression wild.

'Are you okay?'

His eyes lit up as they fixed on her. 'I am now.'

'What's all this about——?'

He crossed the room in two seconds flat, swept her into his arms and crushed his mouth to hers, effectively silencing her, annihilating the need to talk with a frantic, hungry kiss that wiped every sane thought from her mind, let alone the questions that had plagued her for the last few hours.

After an exquisite eternity, they came up for air and she clung to him, needing a steady anchor for her boneless legs.

He'd always had the ability to do this, turn her into a quivering, love-struck girl, but she wasn't a naïve young woman any more.

She needed more than a ride on the back of his bike and a roll in the plantation's hay. She needed a guy willing to accept her for who she was. She needed him.

'I've been doing some thinking.'

'I figured that, considering you tore out of here like a cane burnout was sparking at your heels.'

He grimaced, released her to run a hand through his hair. 'Sorry about that. I needed space. You know I need time out when things get tough.'

'Tough? You ain't seen nothing yet.'

She smiled, while her belly twisted in an agony of nerves. Now he was here, she wanted to shake the truth out of him, wanted him to tell her exactly what he was thinking and put her out of her misery once and for all.

'You should take the job.'

'Oh.'

Disappointment ripped through her, the pain of losing him again cleaving her heart in two.

She'd made the pitch of her life—and failed.

'But only if we work out a way to spend at least six months of the year together. It's going to be hard enough letting my wife out of my sight for that long as it is.'

Her gaze flew to his, seeking some hidden meaning behind his words, not daring to believe her dream could still become a reality.

'Are you saying—?'

'I'm saying this marriage is as real as it gets, Red.'

She let out an ear-splitting squeal as he picked her up and swung her around until she was breathless and laughing and crying all at the same time.

'Hey, don't do that.'

His tenderness in swiping her tears away only made them fall faster and he bundled her into his arms, stroking her hair as she burrowed into her favourite place in the world, inhaling the pure ambrosia of fresh air and ocean and Nick.

She couldn't get enough of him and the thought they had a lifetime together ahead made her light-headed with joy.

'About this marriage—'

The funky tune of her mobile vibrated against her thigh and she fumbled for the phone, switching the darn thing off with a flick.

'You were saying?'

He grinned. 'That could've been important.'

'Nothing's as important as hearing you talk about *our* marriage.'

'Well, then, let's—'

She let a curse slip as the suite's phone rang, loud and jarring, and she laid a hand on his arm as he reached for it.

'Leave it.'

Sweeping a swift kiss across her lips, still tingling from his recent sensual assault, he said, 'Maybe someone's trying to get hold of you? First the mobile, now here? Just answer it, fob them off so we can get to the good stuff.'

He nuzzled her neck and she moaned, trying to block out the incessant jangling of the phone before giving in with a reluctant curse and snatching it up.

'Hello?'

'Ms Lloyd? It's Nurse Peters from the Jacaranda special accommodation facility. I'm sorry to say your father has had another stroke. It's best you come as soon as possible.'

'I'll be right there.'

An instinctive response, a response she might not have given if she'd had time to think, but once it had slipped out and she'd hung up she knew she had no other choice but to go, regardless of her ambivalent feelings towards her dad.

'What's wrong?'

Twisting her hair into a knot at her nape before letting it fall, she said, 'It's my father. He's had another stroke.'

'Hell.'

Nick turned away, but not before she'd glimpsed a flicker of guilt she didn't understand.

'I have to go.'

'Of course. Want me to come with you?'

She shook her head, laid a hand on his arm. 'No, I'll be fine.'

Her hand drifted upwards, stroked his cheek, her heart swelling with love for her husband. *Her husband.* She had the right to really call him that now and she couldn't be happier.

'You stay here, I'll be back as soon as I can and we can talk some more.'

He pulled her in for one last, hungry kiss before releasing her and she hurried out the door.

The faster she paid her father an obligatory visit he'd
done nothing to deserve, the faster she could start the rest
of her life.

CHAPTER THIRTEEN

BRITTANY paused on the threshold of her father's room, focusing on the man that had made her life a living hell propped up in bed.

He didn't deserve this, no one deserved to suffer like this, mind and body wasting away, sapped of dignity, no matter what their sins.

She'd rushed here out of what? Obligation? Caring? It certainly wasn't love. He'd wiped any semblance of that emotion the first time he'd raised his hand to her.

Taking a deep breath, she stepped into the room.

Whatever sense of familial duty had made her come, she didn't want to stay. If he hadn't wanted to broach the gap between them a few weeks earlier, there was no way things would've changed now. If anything, being incapacitated would sour his mood further and she had no intention of bearing the brunt of his temper. Never again.

'Dad?'

She tiptoed to the bed, reaching a hand out to touch his arm before letting it fall to her side when he turned his head slightly, saw her, then rolled towards the wall.

'Go away. Leave me to die in peace.'

The words came out on a croak rather than his usual grunt, shout or bark and for a second a sliver of remorse prompted her to touch him on the shoulder.

He stiffened, allowing her fingertips to linger before shrugging them off.

'You're not dying, Dad. The doctor said you've had another minor stroke with no residual effects.'

He made a sudden move, rolling towards her, and she hated her first reaction was to take a step back.

When was the last time she wasn't afraid of this man, afraid of what he was capable of?

The last time they'd had a normal conversation without his latent temper threatening to explode, she'd been sixteen years old and he'd been teasing her about taking French as an elective at school. It had been the day before her mum had left and the memory stood out as a particularly poignant one as the last time she'd ever connected with him, the last time she'd ever felt safe in his presence.

'What do those old fools know? Pumping me full of heart tablets and blood thinners and goodness knows what. Quacks, the lot of them.'

She hadn't come here to argue, hadn't come to listen to his moaning.

From what the doc said, Darby wasn't going to die any time soon and she could leave him to harass the highly paid staff here and walk away, safe in the knowledge she'd done the right thing no matter how much it stung he didn't give a damn.

'You'll be fine—'

'What are you doing here anyway? Had a fight with that no-good husband of yours?'

His malice-filled eyes narrowed, a nasty grimace twisting his lips as he lifted a trembling arm to jab a finger in her direction before letting it fall uselessly on the bed, and she determinedly quashed a surge of pity.

'Nick and I are happy. We—'

'Happy? More fool you. The only reason that lousy son of

a gun married you was for revenge. Even came around here earlier to gloat.'

Unease gnawed at her, insidious and malignant. She had no intention of listening to the hateful ramblings of a vile old man hell-bent on poisoning everyone around him with his vitriol, but something in his smug grin made her skin crawl with apprehension.

'Hates my guts, always has, ever since we made our little bargain.'

She clamped her jaw shut, determined not to ask what he meant, but her curiosity must've shown for he struggled into a half-sitting position, his expression positively gloating.

'Bet he didn't tell you about our pact. He stopped sniffing around you, I let his stupid old man keep that pathetic excuse for a plantation.'

A faint buzzing filled her head and she took several quick breaths, desperate for air, desperate for anything to wipe the last few moments.

'How does it feel, to come in last in a two-horse race?'

His bitter laugh raised her hackles and she backed towards the door, shocked she'd once loved this man, horrified at what he'd become.

'Yep, revenge, pure and sweet. Mancini must be real happy with your *marriage*.'

He spat the last word and she turned and bolted, clutching a stomach that roiled with the sickening truth.

Nick didn't love her.

Their marriage wasn't real.

This had all been a sick, twisted game to him.

Her feet flew down the corridor and as she stumbled into the fresh air and doubled over with the pain of his deception she promised herself she'd never get taken in by Nick Mancini ever again.

* * *

By the time Brittany arrived back at the hotel, the legendary temper attributed to her hair colour had hit boiling point.

She wanted to pack her bags and jump on the first flight back to London, but not before she'd told Nick a few home truths.

She might have been the good little girl ten years earlier who'd gone quietly after letting him walk all over her, but not any more. This time, she'd go out with a bang.

She could kill him for making her love him again, for causing the incessant ache gripping her heart until she could barely breathe.

All she needed was a reason, and that reason glanced up from his desk and fixed his melted toffee gaze on her as she stalked into their room.

'How's your dad?'

'You tell me.'

She slammed the door, leaned against it when his gaze turned compassionate. She didn't need his compassion, damn it, she needed the truth, all of it.

'Apparently you're so chummy you visited him.'

She snapped her fingers. 'Oh, wait, that wasn't about being friendly. You just wanted to gloat about finally getting your revenge.'

His expression wary, he stood, moved around the desk towards her.

'What are you talking about?'

'Don't patronise me!'

Her tenuous control on her temper snapped as she pushed off the door, met him halfway, placing both hands squarely in the middle of his chest and pushing, hard.

'He told me about your pact, about you choosing Papa over me. I get that family is important to you, but you could've told me, damn you. Do you know how long it took me to get over you? Do you?'

She pushed again, softer this time, a feeble attempt as her anger gave way to anguish.

'Let me explain—'

'Don't bother. I get it. You didn't love me enough then and you sure as hell don't love me now.'

To her mortification, she ended on a sob, knuckling her eyes to complete the pathetic picture with tears.

'Hey, you've got this all wrong.'

He manacled her wrists and she let him, all the fight drained out of her as she slumped onto the back of a chair.

Thumping him wasn't an option, not any more, with concern and tenderness and God-honest sincerity blazing from those unforgettable eyes.

'Have I? Because what my father said made sense.'

Releasing her wrists, he stepped back and ran a hand through his hair, his expression thunderous.

'Remember when you went to Brisbane for a month before leaving for London? Darby didn't know it wasn't a holiday, he thought you were coming back. So he warned me off you, threatened to take the plantation off Papa if I didn't back off.'

Anger tightened his voice, tensed his shoulders as he stalked to the window and braced against it.

'After Mum left, it was the only thing keeping Papa going and I couldn't let your father ruin him, so I did what I thought was right at the time, letting him believe he'd succeeded in ending things between us.'

Damn her dad.

Damn Nick for being right.

She couldn't blame him for his loyalty to Papa, couldn't fault his logic, but she didn't want logic or rationale right now, she needed to vent.

Snapping her fingers, she glared at him. 'Moot point, considering you'd already ended things between us.'

'I didn't want to let you go, Red.'

The sorrow in his tone had her head snapping up to scan his face for proof he was hurting as much as she was.

'Then why? Why did you shut me out those last few weeks? Push me away at the end?'

'You had your dreams, I had mine. We weren't in the right place back then to sustain a relationship.'

His sincerity twanged on her heartstrings, hard, and she gulped as a fresh wave of tears swamped her.

'And now? Our marriage—'

'Was never about revenge, not for one damn minute.'

He strode across the room, dropped to his knees and grabbed her hand. 'Do you honestly think I'd use you like that?'

'I don't know what to think—'

'Then don't.'

He hauled her into his arms and plastered his mouth to hers, obliterating the need to talk, to discuss, to rationalise, obliterating the need to do anything other than lose herself in the magic of his kiss.

But no matter how many times he kissed her, held her, made love to her, there would always be the nagging doubt he'd done this out of spite.

Sensing her wandering thoughts, he broke the kiss, gripped her arms as if he sensed she'd bolt.

'Our marriage was purely business at the start. That was the only reason I married you.'

'And now?'

'Now I want it all.'

She'd wanted to hear those words when she'd first come to him, had first poured her heart out to him.

She'd wanted him to sweep her into his arms and tell her he felt the same way.

But now...

'You still want the same thing, right?'

His desperate gaze searched hers and all she could manage was a slight nod.

But her game plan had changed.

Words were cheap. She'd learned the hard way: the first time her father had called her a filthy name and apologised with empty words, the first time he'd shoved her against the wall followed by more of those meaningless words, the first time he'd raised a hand to her, his pointless words not enough to bridge the yawning gap that had opened up between them.

She'd fled to London, had started a new life. Ironic, as she'd never felt as safe here as she had the last few weeks, only to have it ripped away by doubts planted by the one man she'd never believe and sending her fleeing to London all over again.

'I'm leaving for London.'

His face drained of colour. 'When?'

'Tomorrow.'

'But what about all that stuff you said? About wanting a real marriage? Surely you don't believe Darby—'

'I believe you, Nick, but I have a job to do. I can't just walk away from that. You're a businessman, you understand.'

She played the business card, knowing he'd buy it. Considering the success he'd made of himself, how far he'd gone to cement his reputation, it was the one argument guaranteed to sway him.

Ironic, she would've given away her precious MD job in a second if he'd professed his love a few hours earlier, but what did those three little words actually add up to? Actions spoke louder than ever and right now Nick could say anything and it would be tinged with the doubts her father had raised.

Reaching out to her, he slid his arms around her waist, tugged her close, and she let him.

'I love you, Red. You know that, right?'

The inner girl head over heels for this guy leaped up and punched the air while her mature, sensible counterpart patted her on the head, shoved her down and said, 'Hang on a minute.'

'It's the first time you've ever said it. How would I know?'

He flinched, the hurt in his eyes driving a stake through her heart.

'By my actions.'

'Which one? Where you chose to lie to me rather than tell me the truth ten years ago? Where you married me to get ahead in business?'

He laid a hand on her cheek, brushed her bottom lip with his thumb. 'Every night of our marriage has been real, every single moment I've held you in my arms. You can't fake what we have. And you can't walk away from it.'

'I'm not.'

She dropped her gaze, focused on a tiny thread working loose from his top buttonhole.

'Like hell you're not.'

He released her, stepped away, the tension between them palpable.

'I have to do this, Nick. It's important to me. As to what happens with us, we can work it out—'

'Give me tonight.'

She'd give him the next fifty years of her life if she could trust him, but right now she couldn't get past the doubt, couldn't trust herself around him, let alone anything he said.

She needed time, space. Yeah, as if that would help ease Nick Mancini out of her soul.

He held up a finger. 'One night, our last together for a while. Can you give me that?'

Words bubbled to her lips, empty, meaningless refusals about packing and winding up the local contractors Sell had used and saying goodbyes, but none of them spilled as she found herself nodding.

'Okay.'

Pulling her in for a swift kiss that left her head spinning and her heart a pounding mass of riotous confusion, he said, 'You won't regret it.'

She already did as he strode out of the door.

CHAPTER FOURTEEN

NICK could've wasted time and energy cursing Darby Lloyd but, instead, he put his plan into action.

When he'd initially heard what Britt had said he'd wanted the old man dead, Darby's hatred obliterating the temporary guilt his visit might have caused another stroke.

The old man was vile, determined to ruin his own daughter's happiness. What sort of a father did that to his only child, try to wreck her relationship?

Nick had never been Darby's favourite, especially when he'd started making it big in the district, but what about Britt? Didn't the old guy love her at all?

Something niggled at his conscience, wedged like a spur, digging and needling…something about Britt not knowing about Papa's death.

He'd put it down to Darby not giving a damn about Papa, not bothering to inform Britt about something so trivial in his high-and-mighty world, but what if there was another reason behind her lack of knowledge?

For a woman hell-bent on gaining a promotion she'd travelled halfway around the world to do it, why hadn't she spent more time with her father? A father who was ailing?

He hadn't given it a second thought, happily taking up

every spare moment of Britt's time when she wasn't working, but now he thought about it...

Yeah, something wasn't right and when he'd asked her about it, had mentioned what Darby had said about not giving her any more money because she'd married him, she'd paled before swiftly changing the subject. He could've pushed the issue but didn't want tonight to be about anything other than them.

Staring around the room, he hoped he was doing the right thing.

Would she remember?

Would it mean anything to her?

He'd told her he loved her but it wasn't enough. He'd seen it in every reluctant cell of her body.

Well, he was through talking.

Time to prove their marriage was real in every way.

He had no intention of letting her walk away thinking otherwise.

Unwelcome déjà vu washed over Brittany as she stood outside her father's room.

She'd been a fool to come here, especially after everything that had happened, but something Nick had said about her father niggled.

They'd been discussing Darby and she'd clammed up, not interested in rehashing anything her father had done or said when Nick had visited him.

That was when Nick had dropped his little gem: even though Darby was a nasty old coot, he must love her enough to give her money to start a new life in London.

Just like that, the emotional blinkers blinding her eyes lifted a fraction.

Considering why she'd fled home, headed for the opposite side of the world to escape, when he'd told her she'd instantly

assumed Darby's reason for giving her the money had been
about control as always.

Never once had she contemplated any other reason.

But the more she thought about it, the more it didn't
make sense.

If he'd truly hated her back then as she believed, why would
he cushion her? Why not see her fail and hope she'd come
running home rather than give her money to prop her up?

She had to know why he'd done it.

Clenching and unclenching her hands, she rolled her shoulders, stretched her neck from side to side like a prize fighter
about to take on the champ.

With her muscles as relaxed as they were going to get, she
knocked and entered, striding across the room to the bed,
where her father lay. He looked so old and tired that she felt
a sudden rush of pity, until he looked up and sent her a ferocious glare.

'Thought I told you to—'

'Why did you do it, Dad?'

His upper lip curled. 'Trust Mancini to tell you about our
bargain—'

'Not that. The money. Why did you give me that money
and pretend it was Mum's?'

She'd never seen her dad anything but aloof, cold, angry
after her mum left, hadn't seen him blink when the news of
her death had reached them, and for the first time in for ever
she saw uncertainty cloud his eyes, contort his expression into
that of a confused old man.

He didn't respond, his gnarled hands wringing beneath
the bedcovers.

'Dad? Tell me. You owe me that much.'

She expected him to say 'I owe you nothing' in a classic
gruff Darby response, so she almost keeled over when he
pushed into sitting and beckoned her closer.

'The only reason I let you go to Brisbane for that holiday is because I couldn't stand the sight of you cowering any more.'

He stared at the coverlet, his frown deepening. 'Then when you didn't come back and sent that email you were in London and weren't coming back, I was worried.'

'You'd have to care to worry,' she said, hating the flare of hope she'd finally get some answers to questions that had plagued her for years.

'I cared.'

His shocking declaration came out a whisper and she almost slapped her ears to ensure she'd heard right.

'You call abusing me caring? All those put-downs and shoves and—' She inhaled sharply, breathed deeply, trying to relax. A futile effort, as years of resentment bubbled up. 'You were my dad, you should've loved me! What did I do wrong? Why did you treat me like that? Tell me, damn you!'

To her amazement, tears squeezed from the corners of his eyes and trickled down his wrinkled cheeks unchecked, the sorrow in his gaze wrenching a soul-deep response she didn't want to acknowledge.

He opened his mouth, closed it, before shaking his head. 'None of it was your fault, none of it.'

His low groan of pain had her darting an anxious glance at the heart-monitor machine but the blood-pressure numbers weren't rising and the spiky lines were unchanged.

'I was a monster. What I did was unforgivable.'

'Then why?'

He took a deep breath, knuckled his eyes before fixing them on her. 'Because looking at you was like looking at the young version of your mother I fell in love with. Because seeing you every day reminded me of what she'd been like and what she'd become when she ran out and got herself killed. Because it hurt right here—' he thumped his heart and this time the machine gave an alarming beep '——every time I looked at you and wished you were her.'

She had her answers but they did little to erase the years of bitterness as she belatedly realised nothing he could say or do would make up for what he'd put her through.

Then it happened.

His trembling hand snaked towards her, palm up, begging. She stared at it, expecting to feel repulsed or, worse, fearful, remembering the last time he'd extended the same hand had been to hit her.

None of those feelings materialised as pity trickled through her, pity for the weakened, frightened man he'd have to be to extend the hand of friendship to her after all these years, after all he'd done.

Sadness clogged her throat as she placed her hand in his briefly, squeezing once before snatching it back.

Maybe it was more than he deserved, but in that one, fleeting touch some of her residual anger receded, faded, eased.

'I'm so sorry,' he said, flexing the fingers on the hand she'd clasped as if not quite believing she'd done it.

Needing to escape before she broke down, she managed a brisk nod.

'So am I, Dad, so am I.'

Brittany stepped into the Crusoe Suite, the air whooshing from her lungs as she clutched at her chest, rubbing the sudden ache centring over her heart.

Every detail of the incredible room, from the sheer ivory chiffon draping the open-air French doors leading to a crystal horizon pool to the raised alabaster king-size bed, from the countless tea-lights shimmering in the dusk to the heady scent of frangipani lingering in the air, all screamed he remembered.

He remembered.

Her gaze lingered on the picnic blanket spread in the middle of the spacious room, on the feast of chocolate-dipped strawberries and double-roasted almonds and petit fours, a bottle of chilled Muscato in an ice bucket.

All her favourites, in her ultimate fantasy room.

When had she told him? Their first date? Their second? Their tenth?

Irrelevant, considering he'd remembered her island fantasy and recreated it to perfection in this breathtaking suite.

'I'm glad you came.'

What little breath she had left stuck in her throat as Nick stepped into view, brushing chiffon aside to enter the suite.

If the room was gorgeous, the view sublime, Nick was out of this world. Wearing formal black trousers and a crisp white shirt open at the neck, his hair ruffled by the ocean breeze, he padded barefoot towards her, every step accelerating her heart rate towards cardiac arrest.

'I had to say goodbye,' she managed on a squeak as he swept her into his arms, strode to the picnic blanket and gently deposited her, nuzzling her neck in the process.

'Shh…'

He brushed a soft kiss against her lips, a kiss to fuel dreams, a kiss laden with promise.

'No talk of goodbyes. We have the whole night and I intend to make every second count.'

If his kiss rendered her speechless, the clear intent in his eyes clammed her up good and proper, for there was little doubt that once they'd eaten he'd be feasting on her.

'Here, drink this.'

He handed her a wine glass, his knowing smile telling her he knew exactly how flummoxed she was.

After several unladylike gulps, she cleared her throat and finally managed to speak. 'This must be the most popular suite in the hotel.'

His eyes glittered as he shook his head. 'It's never been booked.'

'I don't understand.'

'This room is never available. It's never been used.'

'But—'

'Tonight's the first.'

Raising his glass in her direction, he said, 'Rather fitting.'

He couldn't possibly mean…he wasn't implying…

'Are you saying—?'

Swooping in for another stolen kiss, he whispered against her lips, 'This is your room, Red. Your fantasy. Surely you know I could never share it with anyone else?'

Her heart swelled with love for this amazing man.

She loved him with everything she had but she couldn't silence the doubt demons perched on her shoulder, whispering in her ears what she'd be giving up, what she'd be risking if she stayed now.

While she'd taken the first tentative step towards forgiving her father, everything she'd been through with him had moulded her into the woman she'd become today: a strong, independent woman too scared to rely on anyone else, a woman wary of loving too much and giving too much.

This room was a fantasy, her fantasy. Was her marriage the same? Started on pretence, built on shaky foundations, something transient, intangible, that could vanish as easily as any dreams she once had for the two of them?

'Why did you build a room like this when you had no idea I'd ever see it?'

He shrugged, his expression delightfully bashful. 'I've built my dreams from nothing. And when you have nothing, hope is a powerful motivator.'

She shook her head, confused. 'You hoped I'd come back?'

'Counted on it.'

His confident smile set her pulse racing.

'I used to come up here for time out.' He pushed to his feet, gestured to the room. 'Did some of my best thinking here.'

'But I only came back for work and we only married out of mutual benefit for our businesses. How could you have known I'd ever get to see this?'

'You would've come back, Red. It's fate.'

'Don't believe in it.'

She made her own luck, had ever since she'd had the sense to flee home and relocate to London. Fate had dealt her a bum hand in the paternal stakes and she'd lost faith in it a long time ago.

Smiling, he held out his hand to her. 'It's the Italian in me. We believe in higher powers.'

So did she at that moment as she placed her hand in his and he tugged her to her feet, where she landed flush against his body.

'I also believe in us.'

She wanted to lose herself in the moment, lose herself in the fantasy, but logic wouldn't be denied. She was leaving tomorrow, wanted to make sure he knew where things stood with their marriage.

'You didn't ten years ago. Not enough to make us work.'

He swore under his breath, hugged her tighter. 'I was young, idealistic—a fool. Let me prove to you how much you mean to me.'

'You don't have to—'

He crushed his mouth to hers, eradicating her protests, her rationale, her reason.

She shuddered as he deepened the kiss, his tongue slipping inside to touch hers, his hands tugging on the sash holding her tie-around dress together.

It slithered to the floor in a hiss of silk, leaving her flesh bare to his exploring hands and explore they did, skimming her skin, his fingers trailing up her thighs, lingering at the edge of her panties before delving beneath.

'Oh…'

She melted against him, clung to him, her need for Nick astonishing in its all-consuming power.

She couldn't think when he grazed her clitoris, didn't want to think when he thumbed it, circled it, backing her slowly towards the bed without breaking tempo.

'Step up, sweetheart,' he murmured, guiding her like a maestro when they hit the dais, gently laying her on the bed, playing her body until she could've sung encore arias all night long.

He kept her on the edge, tormenting her with pleasure as she arched her back, thrust her hips up, desperate to feel his touch, begging for release.

'We have all night.'

He kissed her, swallowed her plea, toying with her until she was incoherent with mind-numbing need.

'Nick, please…'

Finally, he picked up the tempo, his thumb circling her clitoris with perfect pressure, and on the next stroke spasms rocked her body, wave after wave of intense, mindless pleasure drenching her.

Before she could catch her breath he'd whipped off his pants, sheathed himself and was inside her, hard, insistent, demanding more of her than she could give.

She was spent, listless with satisfaction, but as Nick drove into her, smooth and unrelenting, she reignited, tensed and exploded at the same time he did, their cries mingling on the night air before fading away to a contented silence.

She was gone.

He knew it the second he woke, not needing to open his eyes to know Britt had left.

She was a part of him, always had been. He hadn't been

kidding when he'd told her about this room, his hopes she'd come back.

Everyone returned home to their roots at some stage and he'd counted on it. She was the only woman for him and now she was his wife and they loved each other…well, nothing would stop them.

Then why was he lying here, alone, and she was winging her way to the other side of the world again?

He'd let her get away once. *Porca miseria!* Never again.

But he couldn't control her, couldn't hold her back any more than let her go. He understood her drive, her ambition, the same need for success pounding through his veins.

So why the crazy feeling she'd left for good?

They hadn't resolved anything last night. He'd planned to, had wanted to talk, but his good intentions had crashed and burned around the time he'd been unable to keep his hands off her. From there, all bets had been off as they'd pleasured each other repeatedly, all night long, finally falling asleep around five a.m.

He didn't need to glance at his watch to know it was around nine now, the brightness of a cloudless Noosa sky indicative of the late hour.

Pushing out of bed, he wrenched on his trousers, hopping and cursing alternately when his foot caught and he pitched off the dais.

Britt couldn't have got much of a head start on him and he needed to see her, needed to make sure she understood the depth of his feelings before she boarded that plane.

Shrugging into his shirt and caring little for the buttons, he strode to the door, his hand stilling on the knob as a glint of metal on the hallway table caught his eye.

The streaming sun reflected off the object, scattering shards of golden diamonds against the pristine walls, and as he moved a fraction to the left he saw what it was.

His heart stopped.

No, it couldn't be.

Sweeping the ring into his palm, he juggled it like a hot coal, fury warring with disbelief.

Britt had taken off her wedding band, had left it behind.

Which could only mean one thing: she wanted out.

Santo cielo!

Shoving the ring deep in his pocket to eradicate the painful reminder of how much she didn't want him no matter what they'd shared, he yanked the door open.

He wasn't losing her without a fight.

Not this time.

CHAPTER FIFTEEN

BRITTANY fiddled with her empty ring finger the entire twenty-four-hour flight to London.

Had she done the right thing?

With the skin rubbed raw where the wedding band had resided, she forced herself to stop tracing the faint tan line, folding her arms and tucking her hands safely out of fiddling reach.

A good thing too, for if she stopped touching the skin where the ring had been she might be tempted to rub her forehead to erase the big fat C branded there.

C for coward, for that was exactly what she was, a spine-less, quivering coward for yanking the wedding band off in a fit of madness and bolting into the early-morning light while Nick slept soundly.

Last night had changed everything.

She didn't trust words, needed actions, and Nick had proved to her how much he wanted this marriage for real, how much he loved her. With every silken caress, with every murmured endearment, with every soul-reaching kiss, he'd shown her he loved her.

That was when she'd realised she had to run.

She couldn't have left if they'd woken together, if he'd asked her to stay. The realization terrified her. She, Brittany, poster-girl for the independent career woman, was so completely in love that she no longer had control over her own actions. She'd had a final window of escape and she'd taken it.

She had to flee. There was no other way.

Nick knew nothing of the truth about her father, about why that debt weighed so heavily upon her or about how much she knew of the way people who loved you could hurt you.

Telling him the truth would've been the brave thing to do, but just thinking about it made her tremble.

She didn't want his pity or his sympathy. She couldn't rely on that love because one day it would no longer be there. She'd nearly lost herself before—this time she knew that if she let herself fall, there'd be no coming back.

She didn't want him dragged into her sordid family life, didn't want to tell him the whole truth.

This was her past.

She needed it wiped clean before she could concentrate on her future.

Courtesy of a minor catastrophe with the new Phant-A-Sea project in the Bahamas, Nick spent three weeks stewing over his wife's disappearance.

He'd tried calling; she didn't return his calls.

He'd tried emailing; she'd sent him a brief response about how busy she was in her new position, how she didn't have a spare moment, how she'd get in touch soon, yada, yada, yada.

It was a crock, all of it.

How long did it take to tack on 'I love you' at the end of an email? A quick text message 'I miss you'?

While his wife was industriously breaking through the glass ceiling he'd had three long weeks to replay and rehash and remember every moment of their marriage, culminating in that last night together.

If she didn't get it after that night she never would and

he had a good mind to pack his bags, head back to Noosa, bury his nose in business and forget all about their short-lived marriage.

But Red wasn't the only one with a temper and twenty-one long days had served to fuel his fury.

He wanted answers.

He deserved answers.

And, by God, he'd get answers.

Picking up his mobile, he flipped it open, his thumb poised over the keypad.

If he called she probably wouldn't take it, so he'd send her a text of his impending arrival. But what good would that do? Considering the cold shoulder she'd been giving him, she'd probably take off on some piddly business trip just to avoid him.

Better to have the element of surprise on his side.

Knowing his stubborn wife as well as he did, he had a feeling he'd need all the help he could get.

Brittany checked the address on her BlackBerry and squinted at the faded number above the crumbling stone door.

Yep, this was the place.

Some conglomerate she'd never heard of wanted to turn this old Edwardian place in the middle of Chelsea into a boutique hotel. Doing a quick sweep, she noted the disintegrating brickwork, the fragmented window frames and the general dilapidated air of the once grand home; they had their work cut out for them.

But it wasn't her job to assess viability of the building. She needed to wow them with the potential advertising campaign she could produce for a project of this scale, needed a brand-spanking new, bright shiny project to absorb her focus and occupy her every waking hour. That way, she could stop dwelling on Nick and how much she missed him.

Missed? More like craved, an intense, unstoppable, uncontrollable craving that intensified rather than lessened with each passing day.

It had almost been a month and, while she was grateful he'd stopped calling her every day, had stopped emailing her, a small part of her curled up and howled every time she checked her messages or her inbox and found nothing from him.

She'd picked up the phone so many times, desperate to hear his voice, before slamming it down, knowing if she heard his dulcet tones professing his love she'd break down and blurt the truth.

And she couldn't afford to, figuratively and literally. Just a few more months and she'd be free...every cent paid back to her dad and, after that, who knew? Maybe her future had room for a husband and a renewed relationship with her father?

Her BlackBerry beeped, caller ID displayed the new client's number and she read the message.

MEET ME ON TOP FLOOR.
EAGER TO GET THIS MEETING UNDER WAY.

'Damn tycoons,' she muttered, shoving the BlackBerry in her handbag, hitching her portfolio higher and pushing through the front door, not surprised when the hinges groaned in protest.

Grateful the building was only three storeys high, she climbed the rickety stairs, admiring the soaring ceilings, the elaborate cornices and the chandeliers that would be magnificent once restored to former glory.

In fact, the crumbling façade of this grand old dame hadn't done justice to the treasure-trove inside and she could see why someone would want to turn this place into a hotel.

Reaching the top landing, she made for the one open door

at the end of a long corridor, drawn by the light spilling temptingly into the gloom.

Ideas had assaulted her from all angles as she'd climbed the staircase and she couldn't wait to put some of her enthusiasm to good use and wow her potential new client.

Smoothing her hair with one hand, she tightened her grip on her portfolio with the other, assuming her best professional smile as she stepped into the room.

Her client stood in front of the window, making it difficult for her to see, but as he turned and took a step towards her she saw too much.

Her smile slipped along with her portfolio, which crashed to the ground with her hopes of holding Nick Mancini at bay until her work was done.

Nick's first instinct was to rush to Britt, sweep her into his arms and forget the agony of the past month.

That was before he saw the stubborn set of her mouth, the angry sapphire glint as she fixed him with a haughty stare.

He'd flown around the world to be with the woman he loved and she was *angry*?

Thrusting his hands in his pockets, he leaned against the window sill.

'What? No welcome kiss for your husband?'

She picked up her bags, placed them on a nearby table, too cool and controlled for his liking. He wanted her off guard, nervous, so he could bully the truth out of her as to why she bolted, why she'd given back his ring. Instead, she smoothed a too-tight hound's-tooth skirt, tugged on the hem of a matching jacket and perched on the table's edge.

'What are you doing here, Nick?'

'Business.'

'Of course.'

Her slight nod annoyed him as much as her clipped response.

'Unfinished business.'

Unable to control himself, he crossed the room in four strides, hauled her into his arms and kissed her.

She struggled for all of two seconds before melting into him, a perfect fit as always, and he growled, a deep, possessive sound ripped from deep within.

'Don't.'

On the point of deepening the kiss, she shoved him away and if he hadn't seen the real fear in her eyes he would've pushed the issue.

He stepped back, gave her space while the old familiar need to have her clawed at him, demanding and uncontrollable as always.

'Don't what? Give you this?'

He reached into his breast pocket, pulled out her wedding band and, grabbing her hand, held her fingers open while he dropped it into her palm.

'You left it behind, though for the life of me I can't figure out why.'

Her mouth opened, closed, in a fair imitation of a goldfish, and he curled her fingers over the ring before releasing her, not trusting himself to touch her one moment longer without hauling her back into his arms.

'Last thing I knew, you wanted this marriage to work. Sure, you wanted to head back here, and I thought we'd figure out logistics.'

He ran a hand through his hair, rattled by her distant expression, as if she'd closed off emotionally. 'Instead, you bolt before we can say a proper goodbye, leaving your ring behind. Which begs the question. Do you want out of this marriage?'

A taut silence stretched, grew, before she finally raised her gaze to his and what he saw blew his mind: the shimmer of tears, the glimmer of defeat.

'Hell, Red, I didn't mean to—'

'It's okay, I should've told you…' Her words hitched on a sob and he folded her into his arms, powerless to do anything but hold her while the woman he'd seen defiant, sassy and brave cried.

Even when he'd callously shoved her away ten years earlier she hadn't shed a single tear, and he'd admired her for it. Now, as the floodgates opened and she clung to him, her tears drenching his shirt, the tiny crack in his heart that had opened the moment he'd found that wedding band lying forlornly on the hall table widened and he knew he could never repair it again.

Desperate to deflect her tears, he said, 'So are you going to help me transform this place into a Phant-A-Sea or what?'

Her sobs petered out as she sniffled and swiped at her eyes before raising her head.

'You're really going to convert this place to a hotel?'

'Uh-huh. But I'll need the undivided attention of Sell's MD to help me do it.'

'For how long?'

'A lifetime.'

Her eyes widened as she gnawed on her deliciously plump lower lip. 'Are you—?'

'I'm saying I love you and I want this marriage to work, Red. I would've been here sooner but I had to clear up urgent business so I can spend as long as it takes here in London. With you.'

He grabbed her hands, held them splayed against his chest, directly over his heart beating wildly for her, only her. 'It's what I wanted to say to you the morning you ran out. I'll do whatever it takes to make our marriage work, to show you how much I love you.'

Her lower lip wobbled and he shook his head. 'Oh, no, you don't.'

He kissed her, slowly, tenderly, infusing every ounce of his

love for this incredible woman into it, hoping she could feel
one tenth of his love for her.

To his horror, she broke the kiss, wrenched out of his
embrace and backed away, her gaze firmly fixed on her shoes.

'Red?'

When she finally met his gaze, hers was anguished.
'There's so much I haven't told you.'

'Try me.'

Taking a step towards her before thinking better of it, he
held his hands out to her, palm up. 'There's nothing you could
tell me that would change how I feel about you.'

Brittany swallowed a sob.

She couldn't comprehend Nick was here, let alone absorb
the impact of his words.

He loved her.

He was willing to spend however long it took to make
their marriage work with her, here, in London.

He'd followed her here, had made the effort he hadn't
made before—could it be that he really had changed? That
he was offering her something entirely new?

But rather than blurt out the truth, as was her first
instinct, she stalled, searching for the right words, humili-
ated at the thought of the man she loved seeing her anything
less than capable.

'Why did you run? Leave the ring behind?'

'Because this job is everything to me.'

Nick glared at her, his toffee eyes turning icy in the wan
light filtering through the tattered velvet drapes.

'I see.'

From his rigid posture to his clenched hands, tension
radiated off him and she knew she'd have to tell him the truth
to salvage their relationship.

'Actually, you don't.'

Weariness seeped through her body as she slumped into a

stuffy armchair, waving away the puff of dust that arose like a mushroom cloud.

'I need the money. Desperately.'

Realisation dawned as he sat opposite and leaned forward by bracing his elbows on his knees.

'But if you need cash I could—'

'That's exactly why I left.'

She shook her head, twisted her hair into a loose knot before releasing it. 'I need to do this on my own. It's my problem, I'll take care of it.'

'What problem?'

Wincing, she rubbed the bridge of her nose, a futile gesture to ward off the headache building between her eyes.

'My father.'

Nick stiffened as she'd known he would.

'What's he done now?'

She sighed, toying with the frayed edge of the chair's arm before folding her fingers to stop fiddling.

'You know about him giving me money when I left Australia to start here?'

'Yeah?'

She leapt from the chair, started pacing. 'He knew I didn't want a cent of his money. He knew I wanted nothing to do with him. I thought it was all about control. Even tried to flaunt it when I tried to make peace after ten years.'

Suspicion clouded his eyes. 'Why did you need to make peace? Haven't you kept in touch?'

She shook her head, hating the road their conversation had taken, for it could only lead to one destination: full disclosure.

'When I left, I severed all ties.'

'Why?'

'For freedom.'

Freedom from fear, from tyranny, from a father who'd morphed into a monster.

Nick frowned in confusion. 'You moved to London to be free of him and—'

'But I'm not free. I'll never be free until I've paid back every cent.'

Nick shook his head. 'You're not telling me everything.'

He stood, reached out to her, but she stubbornly backed away. 'Tell me.'

'I can't.'

Her whisper faded into silence, finally broken by his exasperated sigh.

'I'm your husband. I love you. I'm here for you, *always*.'

The concern, the sincerity, the honesty in that last word broke through her emotional barriers and she sagged against the window sill.

'He hit me.'

'That bastard! I'll kill him!'

She didn't know what she'd expected when she finally told someone the grimy truth after all these years, but seeing Nick furious, bristling with rage and ready to defend her, she suddenly knew she'd made a mistake bottling all this up.

If he hadn't told her the truth when she'd left, she'd done him the same discourtesy, and if they were to have a future she needed to tell him, everything.

'When I came to you ten years ago and asked you to leave, it wasn't out of some misguided romantic notion. I had to leave. His escalating violence left me no option.'

He swore, viciously and voraciously, clenching his hands as if he'd like to thump something, preferably Darby.

'He changed the moment Mum left. Then when we got news Mum died a year after she'd run off, the abuse escalated. A shove here, a bump there.'

She swiped a hand over her eyes, determined not to shed one more wasted tear over him. 'Then he hit me. That's when I knew I had to get out, as far away as I could get.'

'You should've told me. I would've protected you.'

His cold-as-steel voice sent a shiver down her spine.

'How? You had a farm to run, your dad to help. Besides, I asked you...'

'And I turned you down.'

He swore again, thumped his fist on a table. 'If I'd known—'

'We'd already drifted apart, you'd pulled away from me emotionally, so I guess it came as no surprise when you said no.'

Another curse ripped through the air as he rubbed his neck.

'I'm sorry, sweetheart, I was an insecure jerk who pushed you away before you woke up one day and realised you were slumming it.'

Her mouth dropped open, his rueful grin annoying her more than his ludicrous assumption.

'Since when did I ever give you the idea I was *slumming it*? That's the most ridiculous thing I've ever heard.'

She refrained from stamping her foot, just, as he laid his hands out to her, palm up, in surrender.

'People talked, I foolishly listened. Not that I needed a reason to sabotage us.'

'What does that mean?'

Shaking his head, he thrust his hands into his pockets, but not before she'd seen them clench so hard the knuckles stood out.

'It means I was so cut up about my mum running out on me, I didn't want to allow another woman to get close, really close, let alone love her. When we first got involved I thought you had the perfect family. Two parents, money, everything you could possibly want, while I had nothing to offer you.'

She held up her hand, stopped him. 'It was never about the money. Surely you knew me better than that?'

'I guess I knew it deep down but I didn't want to believe it. How could someone like you love a nobody like me?'

It was her turn to swear and he smiled. 'You can't reason

with a young Italian male, especially one trying to hide his insecurities behind a black leather jacket and a Harley. But I've grown up, wised up.'

He took a step towards her, another. 'I didn't come after you last time because I was too proud and too stupid to risk being hurt. But now it's different, I'm different, and it hurts too damn much being without you, so here I am.'

She'd wised up too, and if there was one thing she'd learned over the last decade it was to fight for what she wanted.

'It's good we've been honest if we're to—'

She faltered, swallowed.

Was she really doing this?

Giving them a chance, ignoring her doubts, ignoring the sterile way their marriage started, ignoring the fear that screamed she'd almost died the first time she'd lost Nick, losing him again if this didn't work would finish her off?

'What?'

'Have a future,' she murmured, her eyes not leaving his, her heart's choice vindicated by the explosion of elation in his unwavering stare.

His exuberant whoop echoed in the cavernous room as he picked her up and twirled her around until she was breathless from laughing.

When he finally stopped, she slid down his body, savouring the delicious contact, the spark of heat sizzling between them.

'Do you have any idea how much I've missed you?'

'Bet it's not half as much as I've missed you.'

She caressed his cheek, her fingertips scraping the stubble. 'I love London, but arriving back here and having to mend a broken heart courtesy of you for the second time sure as heck hasn't been fun.'

'Hey! You ran out on me!'

'Oh, yeah…'

Her rueful grin had him chuckling as he pulled her flush

against him, their hips moulding perfectly and exacerbating the slow build of heat as he traced lazy circles in the small of her back.

'You know I love you, right?'

He stopped tracing circles, his gaze locked onto hers. 'What did you just say?'

'Don't make me say it again, Mancini. Once a day is more than enough. A girl's got her pride, you know.'

'You're in love with me? I mean, I'd hoped, but you've never actually said it and—'

'Yeah, no accounting for taste.'

She shrugged, unable to keep a goofy grin from spreading across her face and her heart stopped as he captured her hand and raised it to his lips.

'I.'

He placed a soft kiss on her palm, his tongue lightly tracing her lifeline until she shivered.

'Love.'

He nibbled along her knuckles, grazing them with his tongue.

'You.'

He nipped at the fleshy base of her thumb, sucking it gently until she moaned.

'Good answer,' she gasped as his mouth covered hers, stealing her breath along with her heart.

His mind-blowing kiss ignited the store of hope, happiness and dreams she'd harboured for so long, sending a surge of longing through her body that took every ounce of strength she possessed not to ravish him on the spot.

Nick Mancini loved her.

Her husband loved her.

She'd finally found the 'something' that had eluded her for so long and she couldn't be happier.

'So you're serious about staying around?'

'Hell yeah.'

He kissed her to prove it, a delicious, desperate, devastating kiss packed with emotion and feeling and love, so much love.

When they finally came up for air, he smiled, the slow, sexy smile that set her pulse tripping as he reached to cup her face in his hands.

'I thought starting the Phant-A-Sea chain was the best thing I'd ever done, but I was wrong. You're my fantasy and there's no one I'd rather live my dreams with than you.'

'Keep that up and you'll have me blubbering again.'

'I love you, Red. Will you live the dream with me? For ever? As my wife?'

He kissed her, tenderly, softly, as if knowing she needed a moment to recover from the ecstasy of hearing the guy she'd loved for ever pledge his life to her.

'You bet I will,' she whispered against the side of his mouth, knowing that, as far as dreams went, this one was the stuff made of legends.

EPILOGUE

'You sure you wouldn't like to elope?' Nick asked, sitting on a suitcase while Brittany struggled with the zip. 'We've got the most romantic cities in the world on our doorstep. How about Paris? Or Venice? Wouldn't you like to renew our vows there?'

'We've had this conversation a hundred times. And the answer is still no.'

Brittany tugged on the zip, wondering how she always managed to pack way too much stuff considering she ended up only using half of it. 'Just move your butt a little to the left, if you don't mind.'

'Like this?'

Nick wiggled towards her with a sexy grin.

Biting back an answering grin, she slapped his butt playfully, letting her hand linger on his firm muscles. 'As impressive as I find this fine piece of anatomy, could you actually concentrate on the task at hand?'

'Hey, I'm not the one losing concentration here.'

He picked up her hand and returned it to the zip. 'Now, hurry up. The sooner you finish, the sooner you get to have dessert.'

Her mouth always watered at the prospect of Nick's cooking, and tonight she had a feeling he'd whipped up one of her favourites.

'Tiramisu?'

'Maybe.'

'You're a hard man, Nick Mancini.'

'Only around you, sweetheart,' he murmured, his double entendre sending an illicit thrill through her.

Heat seeped into her cheeks and she gave one, last hefty tug on the zip, grateful when it finally slid into place.

'You're wicked too. Now, where's my reward?'

Nick slid off the case and hauled her into his arms. 'Right here.'

She feigned indifference, a difficult job considering her favourite place in the world was right here in his arms. 'Dessert sounds more tempting.'

'I'll show you tempting,' he muttered, nuzzling her neck in the sensitive spot at the base, just above her collarbone, until she squealed.

'Okay, okay. You've made your point. Now can I have dessert?'

She slid her hands up his back, caressing the sinews, revelling in the hard muscles beneath her hands.

She'd lived with this man for one, incredible year and, rather than tiring of each other, their love grew stronger every day. How did she get so lucky?

Nick dropped a sweet, lingering kiss on her lips. 'You're insatiable.'

'For food too. Now, dessert!'

Chuckling, he held her hand and led her into the kitchen of her Chelsea apartment, sat her down and made a big show of unveiling dessert.

'I hope this is to your satisfaction, miss?'

He bowed low while placing a huge serving of tiramisu in front of her.

She licked her lips and patted his butt again. 'Oh, I'm very satisfied. Care to join me?'

'Now there's an offer I can't refuse,' he said, slipping onto the chair next to her and opening his mouth for the little piece of heaven on a fork she offered him.

Taking a healthy mouthful herself, she sighed in bliss as the blend of sweet ecstasy burst on her taste buds. 'You really are one heck of a catch. Master chef, billionaire hotelier, plantation owner. Which, by the way, was a master stroke of genius, hanging onto the farm so we can let our kids get their hands dirty when they tire of playing hide and seek in all those fantasy rooms at the hotel. Sure you want to be stuck with little ol' me?'

Every now and then, the fear of the past ten years—the endless, lonely years when she'd convinced herself Nick didn't care—raised its head. Thankfully, he quashed it in typical Nick fashion.

'You're the love of my life, Red. Where else would I be but by your side? Besides, I need to stick around if we're to make some of those kids you just mentioned...'

Her throat clogged with tears, she leaned forward and kissed him, licking a tiny glob of cream from the corner of his sexy mouth.

'Eloping sounds kind of neat, but I think we should head back to Jacaranda to renew our vows like we planned.'

He pulled back, searching her eyes for any sign of doubt.

'You sure? We've made our own memories here. Why not leave the past in the past?'

'The past can't hurt me any more. I made my peace with Dad before he died and nothing I feel now is going to change what happened. But Jacaranda means a lot to you and to me too. It's where we grew up, where we met, where we first fell in love...' She trailed off, blinking back the tears in earnest now.

'I can't believe you actually loved me all those years ago. I was convinced you were only interested in having me along for the ride to London because you were scared of being alone, being the uptight little princess you were.'

'And you'd be the expert to judge, being the troublemaking rebel you were.'

He laughed and cupped her cheek. 'You're gorgeous when you fire up. Always have been.'

'Yeah, well, you bring out the worst in me.'

'And the best.'

He inched towards her, his fingers feathering against her face, caressing with infinite skill and patience. 'I love you. Now and for ever.'

'Now and for ever,' she murmured, a second before their lips met in a burst of sweetness and light and untold promise.

* * * * *

'I'M ATTRACTED to you and don't see why I should deny it. Our kiss in the garden suggests you're not exactly indifferent to me. The solution seems fairly straightforward.'

'You want me to become the comte's convenient mistress?'

'I'm not a comte,' Luc said. 'All I have is the castle.'

'All right, the billionaire's preferred plaything, then.'

'I'm not a billionaire, either. Yet.' His lazy smile warned her it was on his to-do list. 'No, I want you to become my outrageously beautiful, independently wealthy lover.'

'Isn't that the same option?'

'No, you might have noticed that the wording's a little different.'

'They're just words, Luc. The outcome's the same.'

'It's an attitude thing.' He looked at her, his smile crookedly charming. 'So what do you say?'

To an affair with the likes of Luc Duvalier? 'I say it's dangerous. For both of us.'

Luc's eyes gleamed. 'There is that.'

'Not to mention insane.'

'Quite possibly. Was that a yes?'

Gabrielle really didn't know what to say. 'So how do we start this thing? If I were to agree to it. Which I haven't.' Yet.

'We start with dinner. Tonight. No expectations beyond a pleasant evening with fine food, fine wine and good company. And we see what happens.'

'I don't know,' she said, reaching for her coffee. 'It seems a little…'

'Straightforward?' he suggested. 'Civilized?'

'For us, yes,' she murmured. 'Where would we eat? Somewhere public or in private?'

'Somewhere public,' he said firmly. 'The restaurant I'm thinking of is a fine one—excellent food, small premises and always busy. A man might take his lover there if he was trying to keep his hands off her.'

'Would I meet you there?' she said.

'I will, of course, collect you,' he said, playing the autocrat and playing it well. 'Shall I meet you there,' he murmured in disbelief. 'What kind of question is that?'

'Says the new generation Frenchman,' she countered. 'Liberated, egalitarian, nonsexist…'

'Helpful, attentive, chivalrous…' he added with a reckless smile. 'And very beddable.'

He was that.

'All right,' she said. 'I'll give you the day—and tonight— to prove that a civilized, pleasurable and manageable affair wouldn't be beyond us. If you can prove this to my satisfaction, I'll make love with you. If this gets out of hand, however…'

'Yes?' he said silkily. 'What do you suggest?'

Gabrielle leaned forward, elbows on the table. Luc leaned forward, too. 'Well, I don't know about you,' she murmured, 'but I'm a clever, outrageously beautiful, independently wealthy woman. I plan to run.'

*This sparky story is full of passion, wit and scandal
and will leave you wanting more!*
Look for
EXPOSED: MISBEHAVING WITH THE MAGNATE
Available March 2010

Two families torn apart by secrets and desire
are about to be reunited in

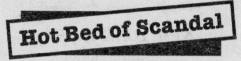

a sexy new duet by

Kelly Hunter

EXPOSED: MISBEHAVING WITH THE MAGNATE

#2905 Available March 2010

Gabriella Alexander returns to the French vineyard she
was banished from after being caught in flagrante with the
owner's son Lucien Duvalier–only to finish what they started!

REVEALED: A PRINCE AND A PREGNANCY

#2913 Available April 2010

Simone Duvalier wants Rafael Alexander and always has, but
they both get more than they bargained for when a night of
passion and a royal revelation rock their world!

Silhouette *Desire*

THE WESTMORELANDS

NEW YORK TIMES
bestselling author

BRENDA JACKSON

HOT WESTMORELAND NIGHTS

Ramsey Westmoreland knew better than to lust after the hired help. But Chloe, the new cook, was just so delectable. Though their affair was growing steamier, Chloe's motives became suspicious. And when he learned Chloe was carrying his child this Westmoreland Rancher had to choose between pride or duty.

Available March 2010 wherever books are sold.

Always Powerful, Passionate and Provocative.

LARGER-PRINT BOOKS!

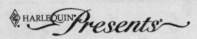

GET 2 FREE LARGER-PRINT NOVELS PLUS 2 FREE GIFTS!

YES! Please send me 2 FREE LARGER-PRINT Harlequin Presents® novels and my 2 FREE gifts (gifts are worth about $10). After receiving them, if I don't wish to receive any more books, I can return the shipping statement marked "cancel". If I don't cancel, I will receive 6 brand-new novels every month and be billed just $4.55 per book in the U.S. or $5.24 per book in Canada. That's a saving of 13% off the cover price! It's quite a bargain! Shipping and handling is just 50¢ per book in the U.S. and 75¢ per book in Canada.* I understand that accepting the 2 free books and gifts places me under no obligation to buy anything. I can always return a shipment and cancel at any time. Even if I never buy another book, the two free books and gifts are mine to keep forever.

176 HDN E4GC   376 HDN E4GN

Name _____ (PLEASE PRINT)

Address _____ Apt. #

City _____ State/Prov. _____ Zip/Postal Code

Signature (if under 18, a parent or guardian must sign)

Mail to the **Harlequin Reader Service:**
IN U.S.A.: P.O. Box 1867, Buffalo, NY 14240-1867
IN CANADA: P.O. Box 609, Fort Erie, Ontario L2A 5X3

Not valid for current subscribers to Harlequin Presents Larger-Print books.

Are you a subscriber to Harlequin Presents books and want to receive the larger-print edition?
Call 1-800-873-8635 today!

* Terms and prices subject to change without notice. Prices do not include applicable taxes. Sales tax applicable in N.Y. Canadian residents will be charged applicable provincial taxes and GST. Offer not valid in Quebec. This offer is limited to one order per household. All orders subject to approval. Credit or debit balances in a customer's account(s) may be offset by any other outstanding balance owed by or to the customer. Please allow 4 to 6 weeks for delivery. Offer available while quantities last.

Your Privacy: Harlequin Books is committed to protecting your privacy. Our Privacy Policy is available online at www.eHarlequin.com or upon request from the Reader Service. From time to time we make our lists of customers available to reputable third parties who may have a product or service of interest to you. If you would prefer we not share your name and address, please check here. ☐

Help us get it right—We strive for accurate, respectful and relevant communications. To clarify or modify your communication preferences, visit us at www.ReaderService.com/consumerschoice.

HPLP10

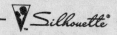

SPECIAL EDITION

FROM *USA TODAY* BESTSELLING AUTHOR
CHRISTINE RIMMER

A BRIDE FOR JERICHO BRAVO

Marnie Jones had long ago buried her wild-child impulses and opted to be "safe," romantically speaking. But one look at born rebel Jericho Bravo and she began to wonder if her thrill-seeking side was about to be revived. Because if ever there was a man worth taking a chance on, there he was, right within her grasp....

*Available in March
wherever books are sold.*

HARLEQUIN *Presents*

Coming Next Month

Available February 23, 2010

HPCNMBPA0210